DAVID HENRY HWANG was born in 1957 of immigrant Chinese American parents. He received his undergraduate degree from Stanford University in 1979 and has also attended the Yale School of Drama. His plays have been produced in New York, Los Angeles, San Francisco, Palo Alto, San Diego, Seattle and Minneapolis, as well as in Singapore and Hong Kong. In addition, THE DANCE AND THE RAILROAD was broadcast nationally over ABC's Arts Cable Network. Hwang's plays have been published in BEST SHORT PLAYS OF 1982, BEST PLAYS OF 1981–82 and NEW PLAYS USA 1. He has directed at San Francisco's Asian American Theatre Company and has taught playwriting at the Basement Workshop in New York's Chinatown. He is the recipient of a 1980 Drama-Logue Playwriting Award for FOB, a 1981 U.S.–Asia Institute Kay Sugehare Award, the 1981 Best Play Obie Award for FOB, a 1982 Chinese American Arts Council Award, and a 1982 Drama Desk Nomination for THE DANCE AND THE RAILROAD and FAMILY DEVOTIONS. He makes his home in New York City.

BROKEN PROMISES
FOUR PLAYS

DAVID HENRY HWANG

 A BARD BOOK/PUBLISHED BY AVON BOOKS

BROKEN PROMISES: FOUR PLAYS is an original publication of Avon Books. This work has never before appeared in book form.

AVON BOOKS
A division of
The Hearst Corporation
959 Eighth Avenue
New York, New York 10019

First Bard Printing, February, 1983

BARD TRADEMARK REG. U. S. PAT. OFF. AND IN OTHER COUNTRIES, MARCA REGISTRADA, HECHO EN U. S. A.

Printed in the U. S. A.

OP   10 9 8 7 6 5 4 3 2 1

CONTENTS

FOREWORD
By Maxine Hong Kingston

"Look here," says a long-lost relative in David
Henry Hwang's latest play. "At your face. Study
your face and you will see—the shape of your face
is the shape of faces back many generations..."
Not only I but many other Chinese Americans
could not hold back tears. There—on the stage, in
public—were our gestures, our voices, our accents,
our own faces. It isn't sad scenes that bring the
tears, but a realization of how isolated we've been,
and a wonder that our private Chinese lives and
secret language can be communally understood.
To see even one other person indicate "myself" by
pointing to his nose makes me know I am not
alone; there are two of us. But to be among an
audience at a play—here are many of us. Here is
a community. We become proud to the bones.

One of the happiest moments I have ever had
at the theater was watching the young men in
FOB pour hot sauce on their food and gulp it down
in an eating contest. I myself had just written a
scene about an eating race. To have a fellow writer
who works an ocean and a continent away meet
me at an intersection reassures me that there is
a place called Chinese America and that I am
seeing it with an authentic vision.

In fact, *Family Devotions,* the most complicated
and disturbing of the plays, has a humor that is
utterly familiar. Let me savor some of it again by
quoting a few lines:

> AMA: ... You remember Twa-Ling? Before we
> leave China, before Communist come, she
> say, "I will send you a picture. If Com-
> munists are good, I will stand—if bad, I
> will sit."
> POPO: That does not mean anything!
> AMA: In picture she sent, she was lying down!

Yes, in the picture my grandmother sent, she was
lying down! We make up stories about the people
far away.

The characters in David Hwang's plays speak
idioms and make sounds that go straight to the
heart and the guts: "Ai-ya." "Suffer, good for you."
"Junk stuffs." That wonderful scene where Popo
"translates" Jenny's speech and comes up with all
the wrong meanings. And here exactly is our view
of the Japanese from World War II movies: "Kill
and laugh. Kill and laugh." "Torture and laugh."
David Hwang has an ear for Chinatown English,
the language of childhood and the subconscious,
the language of emotion, the language of home.

Telling true stories to one another is very important for those whose histories and literature
have been left out of textbooks. Writers will find
these plays appealing because their author deals
with some troublesome basic questions: How to
tell stories and what stories to tell? *The Dance
and the Railroad* and *Family Devotions,* two plays
quite different from each other in their moods and
powers, both tell about people who are shut out

of mainstream cultures and how they manage to create their own rites. In the former play, the dance turns out to be beautiful, but in the latter, the "devotions" become grotesque and deadly. "You don't remember," accuses a character in *Family Devotions*. "Your stories do not remember."

David Hwang writes stories that do remember. Especially in *FOB*, he draws from Chinese mythology and asks what good those myths do us in America. *The Dance and the Railroad* reminds us that when our pioneer ancestors built the railroad through the Sierras, they struck against inhuman "coolie" labor. This play is also about artists who have to support art with hard labor. After work, they practice their art on their own time. Finally, their new art praises the working man.

A good playwright also "remembers" true stories that haven't happened. David Hwang's plays are not just about what is familiar; they take us far imaginatively. In *Family Devotions*, the humor turns black. These are no family devotions I ever participated in. The two most beguiling characters die suddenly and nightmarishly. Is this a warning? Is this what happens to a family that is warped by isolation? Is it time to stop hanging onto shreds of strange traditions somebody brought from China?

Chinese American actors are given too few dignified parts to play. If no playwrights like David Hwang came along, a generation of actors who speak our accents would be lost. A novelist can only invent an approximate orthography. For voices, the play's the thing. Chinese American theater, which started out with a bang—firecrackers, drums—keeps dying out. David Henry Hwang gives it life once again.

INTRODUCTION

American theater is beginning to discover Americans.

Black theater, women's theater, gay theater, Asian American theater, Hispanic theater—these are more than merely fads or splinter movements. They are attempts by the American theater to come to grips with the multicultural character of our society, to portray it truthfully. As such, they represent simply the artistic face of what is essentially a political transformation.

By focusing on the smallest thing, we expose the design of the whole. If we neglect some of the communities which make up our society, our perception of the whole becomes a lie. America has traditionally denied the importance of its minorities, and this denial has been reflected in its theater, which has portrayed a relatively homogenous society, with white males as the centers and prime movers. This is ethnic theater—but the theater of only one ethnic group.

The great American temptation is to be suckered into the melting pot. We somehow believe that to be less "ethnic" is to be more human. In fact, the opposite is true: By confronting our ethnicity, we are simply confronting the roots of our humanity. The denial of this truth creates a bizarre world, cut off from the past and alienated from the present, where cosmetic surgeons offer to un-slant Asian eyes and makeup artists work to slant the eyes of Peter Ustinov, 1981's Charlie Chan.

The plays in this volume are my attempt to explore human issues without denying the color of my skin. The playwright Athol Fugard was quoted as saying, "To me, the curse of theater today is generalizing. You need a place, you need the reality first." These plays spring from the world I know best.

These plays also exist as part of the growing Asian American theater movement. Acting remains one of the professions where employment is blatantly denied on the basis of race, and Asian actors who have hoped to play Shakespeare have found themselves on the outskirts of theatrical communities, forced to be mere ethnic color. Asian American theater attempts to counter this denial of our humanity. The reader who appreciates these plays, and especially those who do not, would do well to examine the work of artists such as Philip Kan Gotanda, Momoko Iko, Jessica Hagedorn, Frank Chin, Winston Tong, R.A. Shiomi, and Wakako Yamauchi, in theaters like East West Players (Los Angeles), the Asian American Theatre Company (San Francisco), Pan-Asian Repertory (New York), the Asian Multimedia Center (Seattle), and the Pacific Asian Actors Ensemble (San Diego)

Immigration is making Caucasians an increasingly smaller percentage of this country's population. This demographic trend will necessarily be reflected in the nation's artistic face, and it seems to me a healthy development. In Hawaii, for instance, where Caucasians constitute a plurality rather than a majority, a work of art is not considered somehow "less universal" because its creator is of any particular ethnic group. If this is what the future holds for American theater, we can look forward to a time when no artist will have to hide his or her face in order to work.

In 1979, I directed the first production of my first play, *FOB,* in the lounge of the Okada House dorm at Stanford University. Much has happened since then, and I am grateful to all those who have helped shape these plays, to my family and friends, from whom I am constantly stealing material, and to Joe Papp, who believed in these pieces enough to expose them to a wider audience. It is to Asian American theater people across this nation, however, that I dedicate this volume. I present these plays as an offering, with respect for the past and excitement for our future lives together.

DAVID HENRY HWANG

New York City
May, 1982

FOB

For the warriors of my family

PLAYWRIGHT'S NOTE

The roots of *FOB* are thoroughly American. The play began when a sketch I was writing about a limousine trip through Westwood, California, was invaded by two figures from American literature: Fa Mu Lan, the girl who takes her father's place in battle, from Maxine Hong Kingston's *The Woman Warrior,* and Gwan Gung, the god of fighters and writers, from Frank Chin's *Gee, Pop!*

This fact testifies to the existence of an Asian American literary tradition. Japanese Americans, for instance, wrote plays in American concentration camps during World War II. Earlier, with the emergence of the railroads, came regular performances of Cantonese operas, featuring Gwan Gung, the adopted god of Chinese America.

FOB was first produced by Nancy Takahashi for the Stanford Asian American Theatre Project. It was performed at Okada House on March 2, 1979, with the following cast:

DALE........................ Loren Fong
GRACE .... Hope Nakamura
STEVE....................... David Pating

Directed by the author; lights by Roger Tang; sets by George Prince; costumes by Kathy Ko; Randall Tong, assistant director.

The play was then developed at the 1979 O'Neill National Playwrights Conference in Waterford, Connecticut, with the cast of Ernest Abuba, Calvin Jung, and Ginny Yang, directed by Robert Alan Ackerman.

FOB was produced in New York by Joseph Papp at the New York Shakespeare Festival Public Theater, where it opened on June 8, 1980, with the following cast:

DALE........................ Calvin Jung
GRACE .... Ginny Yang
STEVE....................... John Lone

On-stage Stage
    Managers .... Willy Corpus
                              Tzi Ma
On-stage Musician .... Lucia Hwong

Directed by Mako; lighting by Victor En Yu Tan;
sets by Akira Yoshimura and James E. Mayo; costumes by Susan Hom; choreography by John Lone;
music by Lucia Hwong; David Oyama, assistant
director.

CHARACTERS
(all in early twenties)

DALE, an American of Chinese descent, second generation.

GRACE, his cousin, a first-generation Chinese American.

STEVE, her friend, a Chinese newcomer.

SCENE

The back room of a small Chinese restaurant in Torrance, California.

TIME

The year 1980. Act I, Scene 1, takes place in the late afternoon. Act I, Scene 2, is a few minutes later. Act II is after dinner.

DEFINITIONS

chong you bing is a type of Chinese pancake, a Northern Chinese appetizer often made with dough and scallions, with a consistency similar to that of *pita* bread.

Gung Gung means "grandfather."

Mei Guo means "beautiful country," a Chinese term for America.

da dao and *mao* are two swords, the traditional weapons of Gwan Gung and Fa Mu Lan, respectively.

PROLOGUE

LIGHTS UP *on a blackboard. Enter* DALE *dressed preppie. The blackboard is the type which can flip around so both sides can be used. He lectures like a university professor, using the board to illustrate his points.*

DALE: F-O-B. Fresh Off the Boat. FOB. What words can you think of that characterize the FOB? Clumsy, ugly, greasy FOB. Loud, stupid, four-eyed FOB. Big feet. Horny. Like Lenny in *Of Mice and Men*. Very good. A literary reference. High-water pants. Floods, to be exact. Someone you wouldn't want your sister to marry. If you are a sister, someone you wouldn't want to marry. That assumes we're talking about boy FOBs, of course. But girl FOBs aren't really as...FOBish. Boy FOBs are the worst, the...pits. They are the sworn enemies of all ABC—oh, that's "American Born Chinese"—of all ABC girls. Before an ABC girl will be seen on Friday night with a boy FOB in Westwood, she would rather burn off her face.

[*He flips around the board. On the other side is written: "1. Where to find FOBs. 2. How to spot a FOB."*]

7

FOBs can be found in great numbers almost
anyplace you happen to be, but there are some
locations where they cluster in particularly
large swarms. Community colleges, Chinese-
club discos, Asian sororities, Asian fraternities,
Oriental churches, shopping malls, and, of
course, Bee Gee concerts. How can you spot a
FOB? Look out! If you can't answer that, you
might be one. [*He flips back the board, reviews.*]
F-O-B. Fresh Off the Boat. FOB. Clumsy, ugly,
greasy FOB. Loud, stupid, four-eyed FOB.
Big feet. Horny. Like Lenny in *Of Mice and
Men*. Floods. Like Lenny in *Of Mice and Men*.
F-O-B. Fresh Off the Boat. FOB.

[*Lights fade to black. We hear American pop music, preferably in the funk—R&B—disco area.*]

ACT 1

Scene 1

The back room of a small Chinese restaurant in Torrance, California. Single table, with tablecloth; various chairs, supplies. One door leads outside, a back exit, another leads to the kitchen. Lights up on GRACE, *at the table. The music is coming from a small radio. On the table is a small, partially wrapped box, and a huge blob of discarded Scotch tape. As* GRACE *tries to wrap the box, we see what has been happening: The tape she's using is stuck; so, in order to pull it out, she must tug so hard that an unusable quantity of tape is dispensed. Enter* STEVE, *from the back door, unnoticed by* GRACE. *He stands, waiting to catch her eye, tries to speak, but his voice is drowned out by the music. He is dressed in a stylish summer outfit.*

GRACE: Aaaai-ya!
STEVE: Hey!
   [*No response; he turns off the music.*]
GRACE: Huh? Look. Out of tape.
STEVE: [*In Chinese*] Yeah.
GRACE: One whole roll. You know how much of it got on here? Look. That much. That's all.
STEVE: [*In Chinese*] Yeah. Do you serve *chong you bing* today?

9

GRACE: [*Picking up box*] Could've skipped the wrapping paper, just covered it with tape.

STEVE: [*In Chinese*] Excuse me!

GRACE: Yeah? [*Pause*] You wouldn't have any on you, would ya?

STEVE: [*English from now onward*] Sorry? No. I don't have *bing*. I want to buy *bing*.

GRACE: Not *bing!* Tape. Have you got any tape?

STEVE: Tape? Of course I don't have tape.

GRACE: Just checking.

STEVE: Do you have any *bing?*
    [*Pause.*]

GRACE: Look, we're closed till five...

STEVE: Idiot girl.

GRACE: Why don't you take a menu?

STEVE: I want you to tell me!
    [*Pause.*]

GRACE: [*Ignoring* STEVE] Working in a Chinese restaurant, you learn to deal with obnoxious customers.

STEVE: Hey! You!

GRACE: If the customer's Chinese, you insult them by giving forks.

STEVE: I said I want you to tell me!

GRACE: If the customer's Anglo, you starve them by not giving forks.

STEVE: You serve *bing* or not?

GRACE: But it's always easy just to dump whatever happens to be in your hands at the moment.
    [*She sticks the tape blob on* STEVE's *face.*]

STEVE: I suggest you answer my question at once!

GRACE: And I suggest you grab a menu and start doing things for yourself. Look, I'll get you one, even. How's that?

STEVE: I want it from your mouth!

GRACE: Sorry. We don't keep 'em there.

STEVE: If I say they are there, they are there.
[*He grabs her box.*]

GRACE: What— What're you doing? Give that back
to me!
[*They parry around the table.*]

STEVE: Aaaah! Now it's different, isn't it? Now
you're listening to me.

GRACE: 'Scuse me, but you really are an asshole,
you know that? Who do you think you are?

STEVE: What are you asking me? Who I am?

GRACE: Yes. You take it easy with that, hear?

STEVE: You ask who *I* am?

GRACE: One more second and I'm gonna call the
cops.

STEVE: Very well, I will tell you.
[*She picks up the phone. He slams it down.*]

STEVE: I said, I'll tell you.

GRACE: If this is how you go around meeting people, I think it's pretty screwed.

STEVE: Silence! I am Gwan Gung! God of warriors,
writers, and prostitutes!
[*Pause.*]

GRACE: Bullshit!

STEVE: What?

GRACE: Bullshit! Bull-shit! You are not Gwan
Gung. And gimme back my box.

STEVE: I am Gwan Gung. Perhaps we should see
what you have in here.

GRACE: Don't open that! [*Beat.*] You don't look like
Gwan Gung. Gwan Gung is a warrior.

STEVE: I am a warrior!

GRACE: Yeah? Why are you so scrawny, then? You
wouldn't last a day in battle.

STEVE: My credit! Many a larger man has been

humiliated by the strength in one of my size.

GRACE: Tell me, then. Tell me, if you are Gwan Gung. Tell me of your battles. Of one battle. Of Gwan Gung's favorite battle.

STEVE: Very well. Here is a living memory: One day, Gwan Gung woke up and saw the ring of fire around the sun and decided, "This is a good day to slay villagers." So he got up, washed himself, and looked over a map of the Three Kingdoms to decide where first to go. For those were days of rebellion and falling empires, so opportunity to slay was abundant. But planned slaughter required an order and restraint which soon became tedious. So Gwan Gung decided a change was in order. He called for his tailor, who he asked to make a beautiful blindfold of layered silk, fine enough to be weightless, yet thick enough to blind the wearer completely. The tailor complied, and soon produced a perfect piece of red silk, exactly suited to Gwan Gung's demands. In gratitude, Gwan Gung stayed the tailor's execution sentence. He then put on his blindfold, pulled out his sword, and began passing over the land, swiping at whatever got in his path. You see, Gwan Gung figured there was so much revenge and so much evil in those days that he could slay at random and still stand a good chance of fulfilling justice. This worked very well, until his sword, in its blind fury, hit upon an old and irritable atom bomb.

[GRACE *catches* STEVE, *takes back the box.*]

GRACE: Ha! Some Gwan Gung you are! Some warrior you are! You can't even protect a tiny box

from the grasp of a woman! How could you have
shielded your big head in battle?

STEVE: Shield! Shield! I still go to battle!

GRACE: Only your head goes to battle, 'cause only
your head is Gwan Gung.

[*Pause.*]

STEVE: You made me think of you as a quiet lis-
tener. A good trick. What is your name?

GRACE: You can call me "The Woman Who Has
Defeated Gwan Gung," if that's really who you
are.

STEVE: Very well. But that name will change before long.

GRACE: That story you told—that wasn't a Gwan
Gung story.

STEVE: What—you think you know all of my ad-
ventures through stories? All the books in the
world couldn't record the life of one man, let
alone a god. Now—do you serve *bing?*

GRACE: I won the battle; you go look yourself.
There.

STEVE: You working here?

GRACE: Part time. It's my father's place. I'm also
in school.

STEVE: School? University?

GRACE: Yeah. UCLA.

STEVE: Excellent. I have also come to America for
school.

GRACE: Well, what use would Gwan Gung have
for school?

STEVE: Wisdom. Wisdom makes a warrior stronger.

GRACE: Pretty good. If you are Gwan Gung, you're
not the dumb jock I was expecting. Got a lot to
learn about school, though.

STEVE: Expecting? You were expecting me?

GRACE: [*Quickly*] No, no. I meant, what I expected from the stories.

STEVE: Tell me, how do people think of Gwan Gung in America? Do they shout my name while rushing into battle, or is it too sacred to be used in such ostentatious display?

GRACE: Uh—no.

STEVE: No—what? I didn't ask a "no" question.

GRACE: What I mean is, neither. They don't do either of those.

STEVE: Not good. The name of Gwan Gung has been restricted for the use of leaders only?

GRACE: Uh—no. I think you better sit down.

STEVE: This is very scandalous. How are the people to take my strength? Gwan Gung might as well not exist, for all they know.

GRACE: You got it.

STEVE: I got what? You seem to be having trouble making your answers fit my questions.

GRACE: No, I think you're having trouble making your questions fit my answers.

STEVE: What is this nonsense? Speak clearly, or don't speak at all.

GRACE: Speak clearly?

STEVE: Yes. Like a warrior.

GRACE: Well, you see, Gwan Gung, god of warriors, writers, and prostitutes, no one gives a wipe about you 'round here. You're dead. [*Pause.*]

STEVE: You...you make me laugh.

GRACE: You died way back...hell, no one even noticed when you died—that's how bad off your PR was. You died and no one even missed a burp.

STEVE: You lie! The name of Gwan Gung must be feared around the world—you jeopardize your health with such remarks. [*Pause*] You—you have heard of me, I see. How can you say—?

GRACE: Oh, I just study it a lot—Chinese American history, I mean.

STEVE: Ah. In the schools, in the universities, where new leaders are born, they study my ways.

GRACE: Well, fifteen of us do.

STEVE: Fifteen. Fifteen of the brightest, of the most promising?

GRACE: One wants to be a dental technician.

STEVE: A man studies Gwan Gung in order to clean teeth?

GRACE: There's also a middle-aged woman that's kinda bored with her kids.

STEVE: I refuse—I don't believe you—your stories. You're just angry at me for treating you like a servant. You're trying to sap my faith. The people—the people outside—they know me—they know the deeds of Gwan Gung.

GRACE: Check it out yourself.

STEVE: Very well. You will learn—learn not to test the spirit of Gwan Gung.

[STEVE *exits.* GRACE *picks up the box. She studies it.*]

GRACE: Fa Mu Lan sits and waits. She learns to be still while the emperors, the dynasties, the foreign lands flow past, unaware of her slender form, thinking it a tree in the woods, a statue to a goddess long abandoned by her people. But Fa Mu Lan, the Woman Warrior, is not ashamed. She knows that the one who can exist without movement while the ages pass is the one to whom no victory can be denied. It is training, to wait. And Fa Mu Lan, the Woman Warrior, must train, for she is no goddess, but girl—girl who takes her father's place in battle. No goddess, but woman—warrior-woman [*She breaks through the wrapping, reaches in, and pulls out another box, beautifully wrapped and ribboned.*]—and ghost. [*She puts the new box on the shelf, goes to the phone, dials.*] Hi, Dale? Hi, this is Grace...Pretty good. How 'bout you?...Good, good. Hey, listen, I'm sorry to ask you at the last minute and everything, but are you doing anything tonight?...Are you sure?...Oh, good. Would you like to go out with me and some of my friends?...Just out to dinner, then maybe we were thinking of going to a movie or something...Oh, good...Are you sure?...Yeah, okay. Um, we're all going to meet at the restaurant...No, *our* restaurant ...right—as soon as possible. Okay, good...I'm really glad that you're coming. Sorry it's such short notice. Okay. Bye, now...Huh? Frank? Oh, okay. [*Pause*] Hi, Frank...Pretty good ...Yeah?...No, I don't think so...Yeah... No, I'm sorry, I'd still rather not...I don't want to, okay? Do I have to be any clearer than that? ...You are not!...You don't even know when they come—you'd have to lie on those tracks for hours...Forget it, okay?...Look, I'll get you a schedule so you can time it properly...It's not a favor, damn it. Now goodbye! [*She hangs up.*] Jesus!

[STEVE *enters.*]

STEVE: Buncha weak boys, what do they know?

One man—ChinaMan—wearing a leisure suit
—green! I ask him, "You know Gwan Gung?"
He says, "Hong Kong?" I say, "No, no. Gwan
Gung." He says, "Yeah. They got sixty thousand people living on four acres. Went there
last year." I say, "No, no. Gwan Gung." He
says, "Ooooh! Gwan Gung?" I say, "Yes, yes,
Gwan Gung." He says, "I never been there before."

GRACE: See? Even if you didn't die—who cares?

STEVE: Another kid—blue jeans and a T-shirt—I
ask him, does he know Gwan Gung? He says,
he doesn't need it, he knows Jesus Christ. What
city is this now?

GRACE: Los Angeles.

STEVE: This isn't the only place where a new
ChinaMan can land, is it?

GRACE: I guess a lot go to San Francisco.

STEVE: Good. This place got a bunch of weirdos
around here.

GRACE: Yeah.

STEVE: They could never be followers of Gwan
Gung. All who follow me must be loyal and
righteous.

GRACE: Maybe you should try some other state.

STEVE: Huh? What you say?

GRACE: Never mind. You'll get used to it—like the
rest of us.

[*Pause.* STEVE *begins laughing.*]

STEVE: You are a very clever woman.

GRACE: Just average.

STEVE: No. You do a good job to make it seem like
Gwan Gung has no followers here. At the university, what do you study?

GRACE: Journalism.

STEVE: Journalism—you are a writer, then?

GRACE: Of a sort.

STEVE: Very good. You are close to Gwan Gung's heart.

GRACE: As close as I'm gonna get.

STEVE: I would like to go out tonight with you.

GRACE: I knew it. Look, I've heard a lot of lines before, and yours is very creative, but...

STEVE: I will take you out.

GRACE: You will, huh?

STEVE: I do so because I find you worthy to be favored.

GRACE: You're starting to sound like any other guy now.

STEVE: I'm sorry?

GRACE: Look—if you're going to have any kinds of relationships with women in this country, you better learn to give us some respect.

STEVE: Respect? I give respect.

GRACE: The pushy, aggressive type is out, understand?

STEVE: Taking you out is among my highest tokens of respect.

GRACE: Oh, c'mon—they don't even say that in Hong Kong.

STEVE: You are being asked out by Gwan Gung!

GRACE: I told you, you're too wimpy to be Gwan Gung. And even if you were, you'd have to wait your turn in line.

STEVE: What?

GRACE: I already have something for tonight. My cousin and I are having dinner.

STEVE: You would turn down Gwan Gung for your cousin?

GRACE: Well, he has a X-1/9.

[*Pause.*]

STEVE: What has happened?

GRACE: Look—I tell you what. If you take both of us out, then it'll be okay, all right?

STEVE: I don't want to go out with your cousin!

GRACE: Well, sorry. It's part of the deal.

STEVE: Deal? What deals? Why am I made part of these deals?

GRACE: 'Cause you're in the U.S. in 1980, just like the rest of us. Now quit complaining. Will you take it or not?

[*Pause.*]

STEVE: Gwan Gung...bows to no one's terms but his own.

GRACE: Fine. Why don't you go down the street to Imperial Dragon Restaurant and see if they have *bing?*

STEVE: Do you have *bing?*

GRACE: See for yourself.

[*She hands him a menu. He exits.* GRACE *moves with the box.*]

GRACE: Fa Mu Lan stood in the center of the village and turned round and round as the bits of fingers, the tips of tongues, the arms, the legs, the peeled skulls, the torn maidenheads, all whirled by. She pulled the loose gown closer to her body, stepped over the torsos, in search of the one of her family who might still be alive. Reaching the house that was once her home, crushing bones in her haste, only to find the doorway covered with the stretched and dried skin of that which was once her father. Climbing through an open window, noticing the shiny black thousand-day-old egg still floating in the shiny black sauce. Finding her sister tied spread-eagle on the mat, finding her mother in the basket in pieces, finding her brother nowhere. The Woman Warrior went to the mirror, which had stayed unbroken, and let her gown come loose and drop to the ground. She turned and studied the ideographs that had long ago been carved into the flesh of her young back... Carved by her mother, who lay carved in the basket.

[DALE *enters, approaches* GRACE.]

She ran her fingers over the skin and felt the ridges where there had been pain.

[DALE *is behind* GRACE.]

GRACE: But now they were firm and hard.

[DALE *touches* GRACE, *who reacts by swinging around and knocking him to the ground. Only after he is down does she see his face.*]

GRACE: Dale! Shit! I'm sorry. I didn't...!

DALE: [*Groggy*] Am I late?

GRACE: I didn't know it was you, Dale.

DALE: Yeah. Well, I didn't announce myself.

GRACE: You shouldn't just come in here like that.

DALE: You're right. Never again.

GRACE: I mean, you should've yelled from the dining room.

DALE: Dangerous neighborhood, huh?

GRACE: I'm so sorry. Really.

DALE: Yeah. Uh—where're your other friends? They on the floor around here too?

GRACE: No. Uh—this is really bad, Dale. I'm really sorry.

DALE: What?—you can't make it after all?

GRACE: No, I can make it. It's just that...

DALE: They can't make it? Okay, so it'll just be us. That's cool.

GRACE: Well, not quite us.

DALE: Oh.

GRACE: See, what happened is— You know my friend Judy?

DALE: Uh—no.

GRACE: Well, she was gonna come with us—with me and this guy I know—his name is...Steve.

DALE: Oh, he's with you, right?

GRACE: Well, sort of. So since she was gonna come, I thought you should come too.

DALE: To even out the couples?

GRACE: But now my friend Judy, she decided she had too much work to do, so...oh, it's all messed up.

DALE: Well, that's okay. I can go home—or I can go with you, if this guy Steve doesn't mind. Where is he, anyway?

GRACE: I guess he's late. You know, he just came to this country.

DALE: Oh yeah? How'd you meet him?

GRACE: At a Chinese dance at U.C.L.A.

DALE: Hmmmm. Some of those FOBs get moving pretty fast.

[GRACE *glares*.]

DALE: Oh. Is he...nice?

GRACE: He's okay. I don't know him that well. You know, I'm really sorry.

DALE: Hey, I said it was okay. Jesus, it's not like you hurt me or anything.

GRACE: For that, too.

DALE: Look— [*He hits himself*.] No pain!

GRACE: What I meant was, I'm sorry tonight's got

so messed up.

DALE: Oh, it's okay. I wasn't doing anything anyway.

GRACE: I know, but still...

[*Silence.*]

DALE: Hey, that Frank is a joke, huh?

GRACE: Yeah. He's kind of a pain.

DALE: Yeah. What an asshole to call my friend.

GRACE: Did you hear him on the phone?

DALE: Yeah, all that railroad stuff?

GRACE: It was real dumb.

DALE: Dumb? He's dumb. He's doing it right now.

GRACE: Huh? Are you serious?

DALE: Yeah. I'm tempted to tie him down so, for once in his life, he won't screw something up.

GRACE: You're kidding!

DALE: Huh? Yeah, sure I'm kidding. Who would I go bowling with?

GRACE: No, I mean about him actually going out there—is that true?

DALE: Yeah—he's lying there. You know, right on Torrance Boulevard?

GRACE: No!

DALE: Yeah!

GRACE: But what if a train really comes?

DALE: I dunno. I guess he'll get up.

GRACE: I don't believe it!

DALE: Unless he's fallen asleep by that time or something.

GRACE: He's crazy.

DALE: Which is a real possibility for Frank, he's such a bore anyway.

GRACE: He's weird.

DALE: No, he just thinks he's in love with you.

GRACE: Is he?

DALE: I dunno. We'll see when the train comes.

GRACE: Do you think we should do something?

DALE: What?—You're not gonna fall for the twerp, are you?

GRACE: Well, no, but...

DALE: He's stupid—and ugly, to boot.

GRACE: ...but staying on the tracks is kinda dangerous.

DALE: Let him. Teach him a lesson.

GRACE: You serious?

DALE: [*Moving closer to* GRACE] Not to fool with my cousin.

[*He strokes her hair. They freeze in place, but his arm continues to stroke.* STEVE *enters, oblivious of* DALE *and* GRACE, *who do not respond to him. He speaks to the audience as if it were a panel of judges.*]

STEVE: No! Please! Listen to me! This is fifth time I come here. I tell you both my parents, I tell you their parents, I tell you their parents' parents and who was adopted great-granduncle. I tell you how many beggars in home town and name of their blind dogs. I tell you number of steps from my front door to temple, to well, to governor house, to fields, to whorehouse, to fifth cousin inn, to eighth neighbor toilet—you ask only: What for am I in whorehouse? I tell north, south, northeast, southwest, west, east, north-northeast, south-southwest, east-eastsouth— Why will you not let me enter in America? I come here five times—I raise lifetime fortune five times. Five times, I first come here, you say to me I am illegal, you return me on boat to fathers and uncles with no gold, no treasure, no fortune, no rice. I only want to come to America—come to "Mountain of Gold." And I hate Mountain and I hate America and I hate you! [*Pause*] But this year you call 1914—very bad for China.

[*Pause; light shift.* GRACE *and* DALE *become mobile and aware of* STEVE's *presence.*]

GRACE: Oh! Steve, this is Dale, my cousin. Dale, Steve.

DALE: Hey, nice to meet...

STEVE: [*Now speaking with Chinese accent*] Hello. Thank you. I am fine.

[*Pause.*]

DALE: Uh, yeah. Me too. So, you just got here, huh? What'cha think?

[STEVE *smiles and nods,* DALE *smiles and nods;* STEVE *laughs,* DALE *laughs;* STEVE *hits* DALE *on the shoulder. They laugh some more. They stop laughing.*]

DALE: Oh. Uh—good. [*Pause*] Well, it looks like it's just gonna be the three of us, right? [*To* GRACE] Where you wanna go?

GRACE: I think Steve's already taken care of that. Right, Steve?

STEVE: Excuse?

GRACE: You made reservations at a restaurant?

STEVE: Oh, reservations. Yes, yes.

DALE: Oh, okay. That limits the possibilities. Guess we're going to Chinatown or something, right?

GRACE: [*To* STEVE] Where is the restaurant?

STEVE: Oh. The restaurant is a French restaurant. Los Angeles downtown.

DALE: Oh, we're going to a Western place? [*To* GRACE] Are you sure he made reservations?

GRACE: We'll see.

DALE: Well, I'll get my car.

GRACE: Okay.

STEVE: No!

DALE: Huh?

STEVE: Please—allow me to provide car.

DALE: Oh. You wanna drive.

STEVE: Yes. I have car.

DALE: Look—why don't you let me drive? You've got enough to do without worrying about—you know—how to get around L.A., read the stop signs, all that.

STEVE: Please—allow me to provide car. No problem.

DALE: Well, let's ask Grace, okay? [*To* GRACE] Grace, who do you think should drive?

GRACE: I don't really care. Why don't you two figure it out? But let's hurry, okay? We open pretty soon.

DALE: [*To* STEVE] Look—you had to pick the restaurant we're going to, so the least I can do is drive.

STEVE: Uh, your car—how many people sit in it?

DALE: Well, it depends. Right now, none.

GRACE: [*To* DALE] He's got a point. Your car only seats two.

DALE: He can sit in the back. There's space there. I've fit luggage in it before.

GRACE: [*To* STEVE] You want to sit in back?

STEVE: I sit—where?

DALE: Really big suitcases.

GRACE: Back of his car.

STEVE: X-1/9? Aaaai-ya!

DALE: X-1/9?

STEVE: No deal!

DALE: How'd he know that? How'd he know what I drive?

STEVE: Please. Use my car. Is...big.

DALE: Yeah? Well, how much room you got? [*Pause; slower*] How-big-your-car-is?

STEVE: Huh?

DALE: Your car—how is big?

GRACE: How big is your car?

STEVE: Oh! You go see.

DALE: 'Cause if it's, like, a Pinto or something, it's not that much of a difference.

STEVE: Big and black. Outside.

GRACE: Let's hurry.

DALE: Sure, sure. [*Exits.*]

GRACE: What you up to, anyway?

STEVE: [*Dropping accent*] Gwan Gung will not go into battle without equipment worthy of his position.

GRACE: Position? You came back, didn't you? What does that make you?

DALE: [*Entering*] Okay. There's only one black car out there—

STEVE: Black car is mine.

DALE: —and that's a Fleetwood limo. Now, you're not gonna tell me that's his.

STEVE: Cadillac. Cadillac is mine.

DALE: Limousine...Limousine is yours?

STEVE: Yes, yes. Limousine.
   [*Pause.*]

DALE: [*To GRACE*] You wanna ride in that black thing? People will think we're dead.

GRACE: It does have more room.

DALE: Well, it has to. It's built for passengers who can't bend.

GRACE: And the driver *is* expensive.

DALE: He could go home—save all that money.

GRACE: Well, I don't know. You decide.

DALE: [*To* STEVE] Look, we take my car, savvy?

STEVE: Please—drive my car.

DALE: I'm not trying to be unreasonable or anything.

STEVE: My car—just outside.

DALE: I know where it is, I just don't know why it is.

GRACE: Steve's father manufactures souvenirs in Hong Kong.

DALE: [*To* STEVE] Oh, and that's how you manage that out there, huh?—from thousands of aluminum Buddhas and striptease pens.

GRACE: Well, he can't drive and he has the money—

DALE: [*To* GRACE] I mean, wouldn't you just feel filthy?

GRACE: —so it's easier for him.

DALE: Getting out of a limo in the middle of Westwood? People staring, thinking we're from 'SC? Wouldn't you feel like dirt?

GRACE: It doesn't matter either way to me.
   [*Pause.*]

DALE: Where's your social conscience?

GRACE: Look—I have an idea. Why don't we just stay here.

STEVE: We stay here to eat?

GRACE: No one from the restaurant will bother us, and we can bring stuff in from the kitchen.

STEVE: I ask you to go out.

DALE: Look, Grace, I can't put ya out like that.

GRACE: [*To* DALE] It's no problem, really. It should be fun. [*To* STEVE] Since there are three of us—

DALE: Fun?

GRACE: [*To* STEVE] —it is easier to eat here.

DALE: How can it be fun? It's cheaper.

STEVE: Does not seem right.

GRACE: I mean, unless our restaurant isn't nice enough.

DALE: No, no—that's not it.

STEVE: [*Watching* DALE] No—this place, very nice.

GRACE: Are you sure?

DALE: Yeah. Sure.

STEVE: [*Ditto*] Yeah. Sure.

DALE: Do you have...uh—those *burrito* things?

GRACE: *Moo-shoo?*

DALE: Yeah, that.

GRACE: Yeah.

DALE: And black mushrooms.

GRACE: Sure.

DALE: And sea cucumber?

STEVE: Do you have *bing?*

[*Pause.*]

GRACE: Look, Dad and Russ and some of the others are gonna be setting up pretty soon, so let's get our place ready, okay?

DALE: Okay. Need any help?

GRACE: Well, yeah. That's what I just said.

DALE: Oh, right. I thought maybe you were just being polite.

GRACE: Yeah. Meet me in the kitchen.

DALE: Are you sure your dad won't mind?

GRACE: What?

DALE: Cooking for us.

GRACE: Oh, it's okay. He'll cook for anybody.

[*Exits. Silence.*]

DALE: So, how do you like America?

STEVE: Very nice.

DALE: "Very nice." Good, colorful Hong Kong English. English—how much of it you got down, anyway?

STEVE: Please repeat?

DALE: English—you speak how much?

STEVE: Oh—very little.

DALE: Honest. [*Pause*] You feel like you're an American? Don't tell me. Lemme guess. Your father. [*He switches into a mock Hong Kong accent.*] Your fad-dah tink he sending you here so you get yo' M.B.A., den go back and covuh da world wit' trinkets and beads. Diversify. Franchise. Sell—ah—Hong Kong X-Ray glasses at tourist shop at Buckingham Palace. You know—ah—"See da Queen"? [*Switches back*] He's hoping your American education's gonna create an empire of defective goods and break-able merchandise. Like those little cameras with the slides inside? I bought one at Disneyland once and it ended up having pictures of Hong Kong in it. You know how shitty it is to expect the Magic Kingdom and wind up with the sky-line of Kowloon? Part of your dad's plan, I'm sure. But you're gonna double-cross him. Com-ing to America, you're gonna jump the boat. You're gonna decide you like us. Yeah—you're gonna like having fifteen theaters in three blocks, you're gonna like West Hollywood and Newport Beach. You're gonna decide to become an American. Yeah, don't deny it—it happens to the best of us. You can't hold out—you're no different. You won't even know it's coming be-fore it has you. Before you're trying real hard to be just like the rest of us—go dinner, go movie, go motel, bang-bang. And when your father writes you that do-it-yourself acupuncture sales are down, you'll throw that letter in the basket and burn it in your brain. And you'll write that you're gonna live in Monterey Park a few years

before going back home—and you'll get your
green card—and you'll build up a nice little
stockbroker's business and have a few American kids before your dad realizes what's happened and dies, his hopes reduced to a few
chattering teeth and a pack of pornographic
playing cards. Yeah—great things come to the
U.S. out of Hong Kong.

STEVE: [*Lights a cigarette, blows smoke, stands.*]
Such as your parents?

[STEVE *turns on the music, exits.* BLACKOUT.]

Scene 2

LIGHTS UP *on* DALE *and* STEVE *eating. It is a few
minutes later and food is on the table.* DALE *eats
Chinese style, vigorously shoveling food into his
mouth.* STEVE *picks.* GRACE *enters carrying a jar
of hot sauce.* STEVE *sees her.*

STEVE: [*To* GRACE] After eating, you like to go
dance?

DALE: [*Face in bowl*] No, thanks. I think we'd be
conspicuous.

STEVE: [*To* GRACE] Like to go dance?

GRACE: Perhaps. We will see.

DALE: [*To* STEVE] Wait a minute. Hold on. How
can you just...? I'm here, too, you know. Don't
forget I exist just 'cuz you can't understand me.

STEVE: Please repeat?

DALE: I get better communication from my fish. Look, we go see movie. Three here. See? One, two, three. Three can see movie. Only two can dance.

STEVE: [*To* GRACE] I ask you to go dance.

GRACE: True, but...

DALE: [*To* GRACE] That would really be a screw, you know? You invite me down here, you don't have anyone for me to go out with, but you decide to go dancing.

GRACE: Dale, I understand.

DALE: Understand? That would really be a screw. [*To* STEVE] Look, if you wanna dance, go find yourself some nice FOB partner.

STEVE: "FOB"? Has what meaning?

GRACE: Dale...

DALE: F-O-B. Fresh Off the Boat. FOB.

GRACE: Dale, I agree.

DALE: See, we both agree. [*To* GRACE] He's a pretty prime example, isn't he? All those foreign students—

GRACE: I mean, I agree about going dancing.

DALE: —go swimming in their underwear and everything— What?

GRACE: [*To* STEVE] Please understand. This is not the right time for dancing.

STEVE: Okay.

DALE: "Okay." It's okay when *she* says it's okay.

STEVE: [*To* DALE] "Fresh Off Boat" has what meaning?

[*Pause.*]

DALE: [*To* GRACE] Did you ever hear about Dad his first year in the U.S.?

GRACE: Dale, he wants to know...

DALE: Well, Gung Gung was pretty rich back then,

so Dad must've been a pretty disgusting...one, too. You know, his first year here, he spent, like, thirteen thousand dollars. And that was back 'round 1950.

GRACE: Well, Mom never got anything.

STEVE: FOB means what?

DALE: That's probably 'cause women didn't get anything back then. Anyway, he bought himself a new car—all kinds of stuff, I guess. But then Gung Gung went bankrupt, so Dad had to work.

GRACE: And Mom starved.

DALE: Couldn't hold down a job. Wasn't used to taking orders from anyone.

GRACE: Mom was used to taking orders from everyone.

STEVE: Please explain this meaning.

DALE: Got fired from job after job. Something like fifteen in a year. He'd just walk in the front door and out the back, practically.

GRACE: Well, at least he had a choice of doors. At least he was educated.

STEVE: [To DALE] Excuse!

DALE: Huh?

GRACE: He was educated. Here. In America. When Mom came over, she couldn't quit just 'cause she was mad at her employer. It was work or starve.

DALE: Well, Dad had some pretty lousy jobs, too.

STEVE: [To DALE] Explain, please!

GRACE: Do you know what it's like to work eighty hours a week just to feed yourself?

DALE: Do you?

STEVE: Dale!

DALE: [*To* STEVE] It means you. You know how, if you go to a fish store or something, they have the stuff that just came in that day? Well, so have you.

STEVE: I do not understand.

DALE: Forget it. That's part of what makes you one.

[*Pause.*]

STEVE: [*Picking up hot sauce, to* DALE] Hot. You want some?

[*Pause.*]

DALE: Well, yeah. Okay. Sure.

[STEVE *puts hot sauce on* DALE's *food.*]

DALE: Hey, isn't that kinda a lot?

GRACE: See, Steve's family comes from Shanghai.

DALE: Hmmmm. Well, I'll try it.

[*He takes a gulp, puts down his food.*]

GRACE: I think perhaps that was too much for him.

DALE: No.

GRACE: Want some water?

DALE: Yes.

[GRACE *exits.*]

DALE: You like hot sauce? You like your food hot? All right—here. [*He dumps the contents of the jar on* STEVE's *plate, stirs.*] Fucking savage. Don't you ever worry about your intestines falling out?

[GRACE *enters, gives water to* DALE. STEVE *sits shocked.*]

DALE: Thanks. FOBs can eat anything, huh? They're specially trained. Helps maintain the characteristic greasy look.

[STEVE, *cautiously, begins to eat his food.*]

DALE: What—? Look, Grace, he's eating that! He's

amazing! A freak! What a cannibal!

GRACE: [*Taking* DALE's *plate*] Want me to throw
yours out?

DALE: [*Snatching it back*] Huh? No. No, I can eat
it.

[DALE *and* STEVE *stare at each other across the
table. In unison, they pick up as large a glob of
food as possible, stuff it into their mouths. They
cough and choke. They rest, repeat the face-off
a second time. They continue in silent pain.*
GRACE, *who has been watching this, speaks to
us.*]

GRACE: Yeah. It's tough trying to live in Chinatown. But it's tough trying to live in Torrance,
too. It's true. I don't like being alone. You know,
when Mom could finally bring me to the U.S.,
I was already ten. But I never studied my English very hard in Taiwan, so I got moved back
to the second grade. There were a few Chinese
girls in the fourth grade, but they were American-born, so they wouldn't even talk to me.
They'd just stay with themselves and compare
how much clothes they all had, and make fun
of the way we all talked. I figured I had a better
chance of getting in with the white kids than
with them, so in junior high I started bleaching
my hair and hanging out at the beach—you
know, Chinese hair looks pretty lousy when you
bleach it. After a while, I knew what beach was
gonna be good on any given day, and I could
tell who was coming just by his van. But the
American-born Chinese, it didn't matter to
them. They just giggled and went to their own
dances. Until my senior year in high school—
that's how long it took for me to get over this

whole thing. One night I took Dad's car and drove on Hollywood Boulevard, all the way from downtown to Beverly Hills, then back on Sunset. I was looking and listening—all the time with the window down, just so I'd feel like I was part of the city. And that Friday, it was—I guess—I said, "I'm lonely. And I don't like it. I don't like being alone." And that was all. As soon as I said it, I felt all of the breeze—it was really cool on my face—and I heard all of the radio—and the music sounded really good, you know? So I drove home.

[*Pause.* DALE *bursts out coughing.*]

GRACE: Oh, I'm sorry. Want some more water, Dale?

DALE: It's okay. I'll get it myself. [*He exits.*]

STEVE: [*Looks at* GRACE] Good, huh?

[STEVE *and* GRACE *stare at each other, as* LIGHTS FADE TO BLACK.]

ACT II

In blackout.

DALE: I am much better now. [*Single spot on* DALE]
I go out now. Lots. I can, anyway. Sometimes
I don't ask anyone, so I don't go out. But I could.
[*Pause*] I am much better now. I have friends
now. Lots. They drive Porsche Carreras. Well,
one does. He has a house up in the Hollywood
Hills where I can stand and look down on the
lights of L.A. I guess I haven't really been there
yet. But I could easily go. I'd just have to ask.
[*Pause*] My parents—they don't know nothing
about the world, about watching Benson at the
Roxy, about ordering *hors d'oeuvres* at Scan-
dia's, downshifting onto the Ventura Freeway
at midnight. They're yellow ghosts and they've
tried to cage me up with Chinese-ness when all
the time we were in America. [*Pause*] So, I've
had to work real hard—real hard—to be myself.
To not be a Chinese, a yellow, a slant, a gook.
To be just a human being, like everyone else,
[*Pause*] I've paid my dues. And that's why I am
much better now. I'm making it, you know? I'm
making it in America.
[*A napkin is thrown in front of* DALE'*s face from
right. As it passes, the lights go up. The napkin
falls on what we recognize as the dinner table*
36

from the last scene. We are in the back room.
Dinner is over. STEVE *has thrown the napkin*
from where he is sitting in his chair. DALE *is*
standing upstage of the table and had been talk-
ing to STEVE.]

DALE: So, look, will you just not be so...Couldn't
you just be a little more...? I mean, we don't
have to do all this...You know what's gonna
happen to us tomorrow morning? [*He burps.*]
What kinda diarrhea...? Look, maybe if you
could just be a little more...[*He gropes.*] normal. Here—stand up.
[STEVE *does.*]

DALE: Don't smile like that. Okay. You ever see
Saturday Night Fever?

STEVE: Oh. *Saturday*...

DALE: Yeah.

STEVE: Oh. *Saturday Night Fever*. Disco.

DALE: That's it. Okay. You know...

STEVE: John Travolta.

DALE: Right. John Travolta. Now, maybe if you
could be a little more like him.

STEVE: Uh—Bee Gees?

DALE: Yeah, right. Bee Gees. But what I mean
is...

STEVE: You like Bee Gees?

DALE: I dunno. They're okay. Just stand a little
more like him, you know, his walk? [DALE *tries*
to demonstrate.]

STEVE: I believe Bee Gees very good.

DALE: Yeah. Listen.

STEVE: You see movie name of...

DALE: Will you listen for a sec?

STEVE: ...*Grease*?

DALE: Hold on!

STEVE: Also Bee Gees.

DALE: I'm trying to help you!

STEVE: Also John Travolta?

DALE: I'm trying to get you normal!

STEVE: And—Oliver John-Newton.

DALE: WILL YOU SHUT UP? I'M TRYING TO HELP YOU! I'M TRYING...

STEVE: Very good!

DALE: ...TO MAKE YOU LIKE JOHN TRA-VOLTA!

[DALE *grabs* STEVE *by the arm. Pause.* STEVE *coldly knocks* DALE'*s hands away.* DALE *picks up the last of the dirty dishes on the table and backs into the kitchen.* GRACE *enters from the kitchen with the box wrapped in Act I. She sits in a chair and goes over the wrapping, her back to* STEVE. *He gets up and begins to go for the box, almost reaching her. She turns around suddenly, though, at which point he drops to the floor and pretends to be looking for something. She then turns back front, and he resumes his attempt. Just as he reaches the kitchen door,* DALE *enters with a wet sponge.*]

DALE: [*To* STEVE] Oh, you finally willing to help? I already brought in all the dishes, you know. Here—wipe the table.

[DALE *gives sponge to* STEVE, *returns to kitchen.* STEVE *throws the sponge on the floor, sits back at table.* GRACE *turns around, sees sponge on the floor, picks it up, and goes to wipe the table. She brings the box with her and holds it in one hand.*]

GRACE: Look—you've been wanting this for some time now. Okay. Here. I'll give it to you. [*She puts it on the table.*] A welcome to this country. You don't have to fight for it—I'll give it to you instead.

[*Pause;* STEVE *pushes the box off the table.*]

GRACE: Okay. Your choice.

[GRACE *wipes the table.*]

DALE: [*Entering from kitchen; sees* GRACE] What—
you doing this?

GRACE: Don't worry, Dale.

DALE: I asked him to do it.

GRACE: I'll do it.

DALE: I asked him to do it. He's useless! [DALE
takes the sponge.] Look, I don't know how much
English you know, but look-ee! [*He uses a mock
Chinese accent.*]

GRACE: Dale, don't do that.

DALE: [*Using sponge*] Look—makes table all clean,
see?

GRACE: You have to understand...

DALE: Ooooh! Nice and clean!

GRACE: ...he's not used to this.

DALE: "Look! I can see myself!"

GRACE: Look, I can do this. Really.

DALE: Here—now you do. [DALE *forces* STEVE's
hand onto the sponge.] Good. Very good. Now,
move it around. [DALE *leads* STEVE's *hand.*] Oh,
you learn so fast. Get green card, no time flat,
buddy.

[DALE *removes his hand;* STEVE *stops.*]

DALE: Uh-uh-uh. You must do it yourself. Come.
There—now doesn't that make you feel proud?
[*He takes his hand off;* STEVE *stops.* DALE *gives
up, crosses downstage.* STEVE *remains at the
table, still.*]

DALE: Jesus! I'd trade him in for a vacuum cleaner
any day.

GRACE: You shouldn't humiliate him like that.

DALE: What humiliate? I asked him to wipe the table, that's all.

GRACE: See, he's different. He probably has a lot of servants at home.

DALE: Big deal. He's in America, now. He'd better learn to work.

GRACE: He's rich, you know.

DALE: So what? They all are. Rich FOBs.

GRACE: Does that include me?

DALE: Huh?

GRACE: Does that include me? Am I one of your "rich FOBs"?

DALE: What? Grace, c'mon, that's ridiculous. You're not rich. I mean, you're not poor, but you're not rich either. I mean, you're not a FOB. FOBs are different. You've been over here most of your life. You've had time to thaw out. You've thawed out really well, and, besides—you're my cousin.

[DALE *strokes* GRACE's *hair, and they freeze as before.* STEVE, *meanwhile, has almost imperceptibly begun to clean with his sponge. He speaks to the audience as if speaking with his family.*]

STEVE: Yes. I will go to America. "Mei Guo." [*Pause. He begins working.*] The white ghosts came into the harbor today. They promised that they would bring us to America, and that in America we would never want for anything. One white ghost told how the streets are paved with diamonds, how the land is so rich that pieces of gold lie on the road, and the worker-devils consider them too insignificant even to bend down for. They told of a land where there are no storms, no snow, but sunshine and warmth all year round, where a man could live out in the open and feel not even discomfort from the nature around him—a worker's paradise. A land of gold, a mountain of wealth, a land in which a man can make his fortune and grow without wrinkles into an old age. And the white ghosts are providing free passage both ways. [*Pause*] All we need to do is sign a worker's contract. [*Pause*] Yes, I am going to America.

[*At this point,* GRACE *and* DALE *become mobile, but still fail to hear* STEVE. GRACE *picks up the box.*]

DALE: What's that?

STEVE: [*His wiping becomes increasingly frenzied.*] I am going to America because of its promises. I am going to follow the white ghosts because of their promises.

DALE: Is this for me?

STEVE: Because they promised! They promised! AND LOOK! YOU PROMISED! THIS IS SHIT! IT'S NOT TRUE.

DALE: [*Taking the box*] Let's see what's inside, is that okay?

STEVE: [*Shoves* DALE *to the ground and takes the box.*] IT IS NOT! [*With accent*] THIS IS MINE!

DALE: Well, what kind of shit is that?

STEVE: She gave this to me.

DALE: What kind of . . . we're not at your place. We're not in Hong Kong, you know. Look—look all around you—you see shit on the sidewalks?

STEVE: This is mine!

DALE: You see armies of rice-bowl haircuts?

STEVE: She gave this to me!

DALE: People here have their flies zipped up—see?

STEVE: You should not look in it.

DALE: So we're not in Hong Kong. And I'm not one
of your servant boys that you can knock
around—that you got by trading in a pack of
pornographic playing cards—that you probably
deal out to your friends. You're in America,
understand?

STEVE: Quiet! Do you know who I am?

DALE: Yeah—you're a FOB. You're a rich FOB in
the U.S. But you better watch yourself. 'Cause
you can be sent back.

STEVE: Shut up! Do you know who I am?

DALE: You can be sent back, you know—just like
that. 'Cause you're a guest here, understand?

STEVE: [*To* GRACE] Tell him who I am.

DALE: I know who he is—heir to a fortune in junk
merchandise. Big deal. Like being heir to Cap-
tain Crunch.

STEVE: Tell him!
[*Silence.*]

GRACE: You know it's not like that.

STEVE: Tell him!

DALE: Huh?

GRACE: All the stuff about rice bowls and—zip-
pers—have you ever been there, Dale?

DALE: Well, yeah. Once. When I was ten.

GRACE: Well, it's changed a lot.

DALE: Remember getting heat rashes.

GRACE: People are dressing really well now—and
the whole place has become really stylish—well,
certainly not everybody, but the people who are
well-off enough to send their kids to American
colleges—they're really kinda classy.

DALE: Yeah.

GRACE: Sort of.

DALE: You mean, like him. So what? It's easy to

be classy when you're rich.

GRACE: All I'm saying is...

DALE: Hell, I could do that.

GRACE: Huh?

DALE: I could be classy, too, if I was rich.

GRACE: You *are* rich.

DALE: No. Just upper-middle. Maybe.

GRACE: Compared to us, you're rich.

DALE: No, not really. And especially not compared to him. Besides, when I was born we were still poor.

GRACE: Well, you're rich now.

DALE: Used to get one Life Saver a day.

GRACE: That's all? One Life Saver?

DALE: Well, I mean, that's not all I lived on. We got normal food, too.

GRACE: I know, but...

DALE: Not like we were living in cardboard boxes or anything.

GRACE: All I'm saying is that the people who are coming in now—a lot of them are different— they're already real Westernized. They don't act like they're fresh off the boat.

DALE: Maybe. But they're still FOBs.

STEVE: Tell him who I am!

DALE: Anyway, real nice dinner, Grace. I really enjoyed it.

GRACE: Thank you.

STEVE: Okay! I will tell myself.

DALE: Go tell yourself—just don't bother us.

GRACE: [*Standing, to* STEVE] What would you like to do now?

STEVE: Huh?

GRACE: You wanted to go out after dinner?

STEVE: Yes, yes. We go out.

DALE: I'll drive. You sent the hearse home.

STEVE: I tell driver—return car after dinner.

DALE: How could you...? What time did you...?
When did you tell him to return? What time?

STEVE: [*Looks at his watch*] Seven-five.

DALE: No—not what time is it. What time you tell
him to return?

STEVE: Seven-five. Go see.

[DALE *exits through kitchen.*]

STEVE: [*No accent*] Why wouldn't you tell him who
I am?

GRACE: Can Gwan Gung die?

[*Pause.*]

STEVE: No warrior can defeat Gwan Gung.

GRACE: Does Gwan Gung fear ghosts?

STEVE: Gwan Gung fears no ghosts.

GRACE: Ghosts of warriors?

STEVE: No warrior ghosts.

GRACE: Ghosts that avenge?

STEVE: No avenging ghosts.

GRACE: Ghosts forced into exile?

STEVE: No exiled ghosts.

GRACE: Ghosts that wait?

[*Pause.*]

STEVE: [*Quietly*] May I ... take you out tonight?
Maybe not tonight, but some other time? Another time? [*He strokes her hair.*] What has happened?

DALE: [*Entering*] I cannot believe it... [*He sees
them.*] What do you think you're doing? [*He
grabs* STEVE's *hand. To* STEVE] What...I step
out for one second and you just go and—hell,
you FOBs are sneaky. No wonder they check
you so close at Immigration.

GRACE: Dale, I can really take care of myself.

DALE: Yeah? What was his hand doing, then?

GRACE: Stroking my hair.

DALE: Well, yeah. I could see that. I mean, what was it doing stroking your hair? [*Pause*] Uh, never mind. All I'm saying is... [*He gropes.*] Jesus! If you want to be alone, why don't you just say so, huh? If that's what you really want, just say it, okay?

[*Pause.*]

DALE: Okay. Time's up.

GRACE: Was the car out there?

DALE: Huh? Yeah. Yeah, it was. I could not believe it. I go outside and—thank God—there's no limousine. Just as I'm about to come back, I hear this sound like the roar of death and this big black shadow scrapes up beside me. I could not believe it!

STEVE: Car return—seven-five.

DALE: And when I asked him—I asked the driver, what time he'd been told to return. And he just looks at me and says, "Now."

STEVE: We go out?

DALE: What's going on here? What is this?

STEVE: Time to go.

DALE: No! Not till you explain what's going on.

STEVE: [*To* GRACE] You now want to dance?

DALE: [*To* GRACE] Do you understand this? Was this coincidence?

STEVE: [*Ditto*] I am told good things of American discos.

DALE: [*Ditto*] You and him just wanna go off by yourselves?

STEVE: I hear of Dillon's.

DALE: Is that it?

STEVE: You hear of Dillon's?

DALE: It's okay, you know.

STEVE: In Westwood.

DALE: I don't mind.

STEVE: Three—four stories.

DALE: Really.

STEVE: Live band.

DALE: Cousin.

STEVE: We go.

[*He takes* GRACE's *hand.*]

DALE: He's just out to snake you, you know.

[*He takes the other hand. From this point on, almost unnoticeably, the* LIGHTS BEGIN TO DIM.]

GRACE: Okay! That's enough! [*She pulls away.*] That's enough! I have to make all the decisions around here, don't I? When I leave it up to you two, the only place we go is in circles.

DALE: Well...

STEVE: No, I am suggesting place to go.

GRACE: Look, Dale, when I asked you here, what did I say we were going to do?

DALE: Uh—dinner and a movie—or something. But it was a different "we," then.

GRACE: It doesn't matter. That's what we're going to do.

DALE: I'll drive.

STEVE: My car can take us to movie.

GRACE: I think we better not drive at all. We'll stay right here. [*She removes* STEVE's *tie.*] Do you remember this?

DALE: What—you think I borrow clothes or something? Hell, I don't even wear ties.

[GRACE *takes the tie, wraps it around* DALE's *face like a blindfold.*]

DALE: Grace, what are you...?

GRACE: [*To* STEVE] Do you remember this?

DALE: I already told you. I don't need a closer look or nothing.

STEVE: Yes.

GRACE: [*Ties the blindfold, releases it*] Let's sit down.

DALE: Wait.

STEVE: You want me to sit here?

DALE: Grace, is he understanding you?

GRACE: Have you ever played Group Story?

STEVE: Yes, I have played that.

DALE: There—there he goes again! Grace, I'm gonna take...

[*He starts to remove the blindfold.*]

GRACE: [*Stopping him*] Dale, listen or you won't understand.

DALE: But how come *he's* understanding?

GRACE: Because he's listening.

DALE: But...

GRACE: Now, let's play Group Story.

DALE: Not again. Grace, that's only good when you're stoned.

GRACE: Who wants to start? Steve, you know the rules?

STEVE: Yes—I understand.

DALE: See, we're talking normal speed—and he still understood.

GRACE: Dale, would you like to start?

[*Pause.*]

DALE: All right.

[*By this time, the* LIGHTS HAVE DIMMED, *throwing shadows on the stage.* GRACE *will strike two pots together to indicate each speaker change and the ritual will gradually take on elements of Chinese opera.*]

Uh, once upon a time...there were...three

bears—Grace, this is ridiculous!

GRACE: Tell a story.

DALE: ...three bears and they each had...cancer of the lymph nodes. Uh—and they were very sad. So the baby bear said, "I'll go to the new Cedar Sinai Hospital, where they may have a cure for this fatal illness."

GRACE: But the new Cedar Sinai Hospital happened to be two thousand miles away—across the ocean.

STEVE: [*Gradually losing his accent*] That is very far.

DALE: How did—? So, the bear tried to swim over, but his leg got chewed off by alligators—are there alligators in the Pacific Ocean?—Oh, well. So he ended up having to go for a leg *and* a cure for malignant cancer of the lymph nodes.

GRACE: When he arrived there, he came face to face with—

STEVE: With Gwan Gung, god of warriors, writers, and prostitutes.

DALE: And Gwan Gung looked at the bear and said...

GRACE: ...strongly and with spirit...

STEVE: "One-legged bear, what are you doing on my land? You are from America, are you not?"

DALE: And the bear said, "Yes. Yes."

GRACE: And Gwan Gung replied...

STEVE: [*Getting up*] By stepping forward, sword drawn, ready to wound, not kill, not end it so soon. To draw it out, play it, taunt it, make it feel like a dog.

DALE: Which is probably rather closely related to the bear.

GRACE: Gwan Gung said—

STEVE: "When I came to America, did you lick my
wounds? When I came to America, did you cure
my sickness?"

DALE: And just as Gwan Gung was about to
strike—

GRACE: There arrived Fa Mu Lan, the Woman
Warrior. [*She stands, faces* STEVE. *From here
on in, striking pots together is not needed.*]
"Gwan Gung."

STEVE: "What do you want? Don't interfere! Don't
forget, I have gone before you into battle many
times."

DALE: But Fa Mu Lan seemed not to hear Gwan
Gung's warning. She stood between him and
the bear, drawing out her own sword.

GRACE: "You will learn I cannot forget. I don't forget, Gwan Gung. Spare the bear and I will present gifts."

STEVE: "Very well. He is hardly worth killing."

DALE: And the bear hopped off. Fa Mu Lan pulled
a parcel from beneath her gown. [*She removes*
DALE's *blindfold.*]

DALE: She pulled out two items.

GRACE: "This is for you." [*She hands blindfold to*
STEVE.]

STEVE: "What is that?"

DALE: She showed him a beautiful piece of red silk,
thick enough to be opaque, yet so light, he barely
felt it in his hands.

GRACE: "Do you remember this?"

STEVE: "Why, yes. I used this silk for sport one
day. How did you get hold of it?"

DALE: Then she presented him with a second item.
It was a fabric—thick and dried and brittle.

GRACE: "Do you remember this?"

STEVE: [*Turning away*] "No, no. I've never seen this before in my life. This has nothing to do with me. What is it—a dragon skin?"

DALE: Fa Mu Lan handed it to Gwan Gung.

GRACE: "Never mind. Use it—as a tablecloth. As a favor to me."

STEVE: "It's much too hard and brittle. But, to show you my graciousness in receiving—I will use it tonight!

DALE: That night, Gwan Gung had a large banquet, at which there was plenty, even for the slaves. But Fa Mu Lan ate nothing. She waited until midnight, till Gwan Gung and the gods were full of wine and empty of sense. Sneaking behind him, she pulled out the tablecloth, waving it above her head.

GRACE: [*Ripping the tablecloth from the table*] "Gwan Gung, you foolish boy. This thing you have used tonight as a tablecloth—it is the stretched and dried skins of my fathers. My fathers, whom you slew—for sport! And you have been eating their sins—you ate them!"

STEVE: "No. I was blindfolded. I did not know."

DALE: Fa Mu Lan waved the skin before Gwan Gung's face. It smelled suddenly of death.

GRACE: "Remember the day you played? Remember? Well, eat that day, Gwan Gung."

STEVE: "I am not responsible. No. No."

[GRACE *throws one end of the tablecloth to* DALE, *who catches it. Together, they become like* STEVE'*s parents. They chase him about the stage, waving the tablecloth like a net.*]

DALE: Yes!

GRACE: Yes!

STEVE: No!

DALE: You must!

GRACE: Go!

STEVE: Where?

DALE: To America!

GRACE: To work!

STEVE: Why?

DALE: Because!

GRACE: We need!

STEVE: No!

DALE: Why?

GRACE: Go.

STEVE: Hard!

DALE: So?

GRACE: Need.

STEVE: Far!

DALE: So?

GRACE: Need!

STEVE: Safe!

DALE: Here?

GRACE: No!

STEVE: Why?

DALE: Them.
  [*Points.*]

GRACE: Them.
  [*Points.*]

STEVE: Won't!

DALE: Must!

GRACE: Must!

STEVE: Won't!

DALE: Go!

GRACE: Go!

STEVE: Won't!

DALE: Bye!

GRACE: Bye!

STEVE: Won't!

DALE: Fare!

GRACE: Well!

[DALE *and* GRACE *drop the tablecloth over* STEVE, *who sinks to the floor.* GRACE *then moves off-stage, into the bathroom—storage room, while* DALE *goes upstage and stands with his back to the audience. Silence.*]

STEVE: [*Begins pounding the ground*] Noooo! [*He throws off the tablecloth, standing up full.* LIGHTS UP FULL, *blindingly.*] I am GWAN GUNG!

DALE: [*Turning downstage suddenly*] What...?

STEVE: I HAVE COME TO THIS LAND TO STUDY!

DALE: Grace...

STEVE: TO STUDY THE ARTS OF WAR, OF LITERATURE, OF RIGHTEOUSNESS!

DALE: A movie's fine.

STEVE: I FOUGHT THE WARS OF THE THREE KINGDOMS!

DALE: An ordinary movie, let's go.

STEVE: I FOUGHT WITH THE FIRST PI-ONEERS, THE FIRST WARRIORS THAT CHOSE TO FOLLOW THE WHITE GHOSTS TO THIS LAND!

DALE: You can pick okay?

STEVE: I WAS THEIR HERO, THEIR LEADER, THEIR FIRE!

DALE: I'll even let him drive, how's that?

STEVE: AND THIS LAND IS MINE! IT HAS NO RIGHT TO TREAT ME THIS WAY!

GRACE: No. Gwan Gung, *you* have no rights.

STEVE: Who's speaking?

GRACE: [*Enters with a* da dao *and* mao, *two swords*] It is Fa Mu Lan. You are in a new land, Gwan Gung.

STEVE: Not new—I have been here before, many times. This time, I said I will have it easy. I will come as no ChinaMan before—on a plane, with money and rank.

GRACE: And?

STEVE: And—there is no change. I am still treated like this! This land...has no right. I AM GWAN GUNG!

GRACE: And I am Fa Mu Lan.

DALE: I'll be Chiang Kai-shek, how's that?

STEVE: [*To* DALE] You! How can you—? I came over with your parents.

GRACE: [*Turning to* STEVE] We are in America. And we have a battle to fight.

[*She tosses the* da dao *to* STEVE. *They square off.*]

STEVE: I don't want to fight you.

GRACE: You killed my family.

STEVE: You were revenged—I ate your father's sins.

GRACE: That's not revenge!

[*Swords strike.*]

GRACE: That was only the tease.

[*Strike.*]

GRACE: What's the point in dying if you don't know the cause of your death?

[*Series of strikes.* STEVE *falls.*]

DALE: Okay! That's it!

[GRACE *stands over* STEVE, *her sword pointed at his heart.* DALE *snatches the sword from her hands. She does not move.*]

DALE: Jesus! Enough is enough!

[DALE *takes* STEVE's *sword; he also does not react.*]

DALE: What the hell kind of movie was that?

[DALE *turns his back on the couple, heads for the bathroom—storage room.* GRACE *uses her now-invisible sword to thrust in and out of* STEVE'*s heart once.*]

DALE: That's it. Game's over. Now just sit down here. Breathe. One. Two. One. Two. Air. Good stuff. Glad they made it. Right, cousin?

[DALE *strokes* GRACE'*s hair. They freeze.* STEVE *rises slowly to his knees and delivers a monologue to the audience.*]

STEVE: Ssssh! Please, miss! Please—quiet! I will not hurt you, I promise. All I want is... food... anything. You look full of plenty. I have not eaten almost one week now, but four days past when I found one egg and I ate every piece of it—including shell. Every piece, I ate. Please. Don't you have anything extra? [*Pause*] I want to. Now. This land does not want us any more than China. But I cannot. All work was done, then the bosses said they could not send us back. And I am running, running from Eureka, running from San Francisco, running from Los Angeles. And I been eating very little. One egg, only. [*Pause*] All America wants ChinaMen go home, but no one want it bad enough to pay our way. Now, please, can't you give even little? [*Pause*] I ask you, what you hate most? What work most awful for white woman? [*Pause*] Good. I will do that thing for you—you can give me food. [*Pause*] Think—you relax, you are given those things, clean, dry, press. No scrub, no dry. It is wonderful thing I offer you. [*Pause*] Good. Give me those and please bring food, or I be done before these things.

[GRACE *steps away from* DALE *with box.*]

GRACE: Here—I've brought you something. [*She hands him the box.*] Open it.

[*He hesitates, then does, and takes out a small* chong you bing.]

GRACE: Eat it.

[*He does, slowly at first, then ravenously.*]

GRACE: Good. Eat it all down. It's just food. Really. Feel better now? Good. Eat the *bing*. Hold it in your hands. Your hands...are beautiful. Lift it to your mouth. Your mouth...is beautiful. Bite it with your teeth. Your teeth...are beautiful. Crush it with your tongue. Your tongue...is beautiful. Slide it down your throat. Your throat...is beautiful.

STEVE: Our hands are beautiful.

[*She holds hers next to his.*]

GRACE: What do you see?

STEVE: I see...I see the hands of warriors.

GRACE: Warriors? What of gods then?

STEVE: There are no gods that travel. Only warriors travel. [*Silence*] Would you like go dance?

GRACE: Yeah. Okay. Sure.

[*They start to leave.* DALE *speaks softly.*]

DALE: Well, if you want to be alone...

GRACE: I think we would, Dale. Is that okay? [*Pause*] Thanks for coming over. I'm sorry things got so screwed up.

DALE: Oh—uh—that's okay. The evening was real...different, anyway.

GRACE: Yeah. Maybe you can take Frank off the tracks now?

DALE: [*laughing softly*] Yeah. Maybe I will.

STEVE: [*To* DALE] Very nice meeting you. [*Extends his hand*]

DALE: [*Does not take it*] Yeah. Same here.

[STEVE *and* GRACE *start to leave.*]

DALE: You know...I think you picked up English faster than anyone I've ever met.

[*Pause.*]

STEVE: Thank you.

GRACE: See you.

STEVE: Good-bye.

DALE: Bye.

[GRACE *and* STEVE *exit.*]

CODA

DALE *alone in the back room. He examines the swords, the tablecloth, the box. He sits down.*

DALE: F-O-B. Fresh Off the Boat. FOB. Clumsy, ugly, greasy FOB. Loud, stupid, four-eyed FOB. Big feet. Horny. Like Lenny in *Of Mice and Men*. F-O-B. Fresh Off the Boat. FOB.

SLOW FADE TO BLACK

THE DANCE
AND THE RAILROAD

For John and Tzi

This play was commissioned by the New Federal
Theater under a grant from the U.S. Department
of Education. Special thanks to Jack Tchen and
the New York Chinatown History Project, and
Genny Chomori of the UCLA Asian American
Studies Center.

The Dance and the Railroad was first produced
by the Henry Street Settlement's New Federal
Theater, Woodie King, Jr., and Steve Tennen, pro-
ducers. It opened on March 25, 1981, with the
following cast:

LONE....................... John Lone
MA .... Tzi Ma
Alternate Actor .... Glenn Kubota

Directed by John Lone. Sculpture by Andrea
Zakin, lights by Grant Ornstein, costumes by Judy
Dearing; Alice Jankowiak was production stage
manager; music and choreography by John Lone.

It was then produced by Joseph Papp at the New York Shakespeare Festival Public Theater, where it opened at the Anspacher Theater on July 16, 1981, with the following cast:

LONE........................ John Lone
MA .... Tzi Ma
Alternate Actor .... Toshi Toda

Directed by John Lone; setting by Karen Schulz; lights by Victor En Yu Tan; costumes by Judy Dearing; music and choreography by John Lone. Alice Jankowiak was production stage manager.

CHARACTERS

LONE, twenty years old, ChinaMan railroad
   worker.
MA, eighteen years old, ChinaMan railroad worker.

PLACE

A mountaintop near the transcontinental railroad.

TIME

June, 1867.

SYNOPSIS OF SCENES

Scene 1. Afternoon.
Scene 2. Afternoon, a day later.
Scene 3. Late afternoon, four days later.
Scene 4. Late that night.
Scene 5. Just before the following dawn.

Scene 1

A mountaintop. LONE *is practicing opera steps. He swings his pigtail around like a fan.* MA *enters, cautiously, watches from a hidden spot.* MA *approaches* LONE.

LONE: So, there are insects hiding in the bushes.
MA: Hey, listen, we haven't met, but—
LONE: I don't spend time with insects.
    [LONE *whips his hair into* MA's *face;* MA *backs off;* LONE *pursues him, swiping at* MA *with his hair.*]
MA: What the—? Cut it out!
    [MA *pushes* LONE *away.*]
LONE: Don't push me.
MA: What was that for?
LONE: Don't ever push me again.
MA: You mess like that, you're gonna get pushed.
LONE: Don't push me.
MA: You started it. I just wanted to watch.
LONE: You "just wanted to watch." Did you ask my permission?
MA: What?
LONE: Did you?
MA: C'mon.
LONE: You can't expect to get in for free.

MA: Listen. I got some stuff you'll wanna hear.

LONE: You think so?

MA: Yeah. Some advice.

LONE: Advice? How old are you, anyway?

MA: Eighteen.

LONE: A child.

MA: Yeah. Right. A child. But listen—

LONE: A child who tries to advise a grown man—

MA: Listen, you got this kind of attitude.

LONE: —is a child who will never grow up.

MA: You know, the ChinaMen down at camp, they can't stand it.

LONE: Oh?

MA: Yeah. You gotta watch yourself. You know what they say? They call you "Prince of the Mountain." Like you're too good to spend time with them.

LONE: Perceptive of them.

MA: After all, you never sing songs, never tell stories. They say you act like your spit is too clean for them, and they got ways to fix that.

LONE: Is that so?

MA: Like they're gonna bury you in the shit buckets, so you'll have more to clean than your nails.

LONE: But I don't shit.

MA: Or they're gonna cut out your tongue, since you never speak to them.

LONE: There's no one here worth talking to.

MA: Cut it out, Lone. Look, I'm trying to help you, all right? I got a solution.

LONE: So young yet so clever.

MA: That stuff you're doing—it's beautiful. Why don't you do it for the guys at camp? Help us celebrate?

LONE: What will "this stuff" help celebrate?

MA: C'mon. The strike, of course. Guys on a railroad gang, we gotta stick together, you know.

LONE: This is something to celebrate?

MA: Yeah. Yesterday, the weak-kneed ChinaMen, they were running around like chickens without a head: "The white devils are sending their soldiers! Shoot us all!" But now, look—day four, see? Still in one piece. Those soldiers—we've never seen a gun or a bullet.

LONE: So you're all warrior-spirits, huh?

MA: They're scared of us, Lone—that's what it means.

LONE: I appreciate your advice. Tell you what— you go down—

MA: Yeah?

LONE: Down to the camp—

MA: Okay.

LONE: To where the men are—

MA: Yeah?

LONE: Sit there—

MA: Yeah?

LONE: And wait for me.

MA: Okay.

[*Pause.*]

That's it? What do you think I am?

LONE: I think you're an insect interrupting my practice. So fly away. Go home.

MA: Look, I didn't come here to get laughed at.

LONE: No, I suppose you didn't.

MA: So just stay up here. By yourself. You deserve it.

LONE: I do.

MA: And don't expect any more help from me.

LONE: I haven't gotten any yet.

MA: If one day, you wake up and your head is buried in the shit can—

LONE: Yes?

MA: You can't find your body, your tongue is cut
out—

LONE: Yes.

MA: Don't worry, 'cuz I'll be there.

LONE: Oh.

MA: To make sure your mother's head is sitting
right next to yours.
    [MA *exits*.]

LONE: His head is too big for this mountain. [*Returns to practicing*]

Scene 2

Mountaintop. Next day. LONE *is practicing.* MA *enters.*

MA: Hey.

LONE: You? Again?

MA: I forgive you.

LONE: You...what?

MA: For making fun of me yesterday. I forgive you.

LONE: You can't—

MA: No. Don't thank me.

LONE: You can't forgive me.

MA: No. Don't mention it.

LONE: You—! I never asked for your forgiveness.

MA: I know. That's just the kinda guy I am.

LONE: This is ridiculous. Why don't you leave? Go down to your friends and play soldiers, sing songs, tell stories.

MA: Ah! See? That's just it. I got other ways I wanna spend my time. Will you teach me the opera?

LONE: What?

MA: I wanna learn it. I dreamt about it all last night.

LONE: No.

MA: The dance, the opera—I can do it.

LONE: You think so?

MA: Yeah. When I get outa here, I wanna go back to China and perform.

LONE: You want to become an actor?

MA: Well, I wanna perform.

LONE: Don't you remember the story about the three sons whose parents send them away to learn a trade? After three years, they return. The first one says, "I have become a copper-smith." The parents say, "Good. Second son, what have you become?" "I've become a silver-smith." "Good—and youngest son, what about you?" "I have become an actor." When the parents hear that their son has become only an actor, they are very sad. The mother beats her head against the ground until the ground, out of pity, opens up and swallows her. The father is so angry he can't even speak, and the anger builds up inside him until it blows his body to pieces—little bits of his skin are found hanging from trees days later. You don't know how you endanger your relatives by becoming an actor.

MA: Well, I don't wanna become an "actor." That sounds terrible. I just wanna perform. Look, I'll be rich by the time I get out of here, right?

LONE: Oh?

MA: Sure. By the time I go back to China, I'll ride in gold sedan chairs, with twenty wives fanning me all around.

LONE: Twenty wives? This boy is ambitious.

MA: I'll give out pigs on New Year's and keep a stable of small birds to give to any woman who pleases me. And in my spare time, I'll perform.

LONE: Between your twenty wives and your birds, where will you find a free moment?

MA: I'll play Gwan Gung and tell stories of what life was like on the Gold Mountain.

LONE: Ma, just how long have you been in "America"?

MA: Huh? About four weeks.

LONE: You are a big dreamer.

MA: Well, all us ChinaMen here are—right? Men with little dreams—have little brains to match. They walk with their eyes down, trying to find extra grains of rice on the ground.

LONE: So, you know all about "America"? Tell me, what kind of stories will you tell?

MA: I'll say, "We laid tracks like soldiers. Mountains? We hung from cliffs in baskets and the winds blew us like birds. Snow? We lived underground like moles for days at a time. Deserts? We—"

LONE: Wait. Wait. How do you know these things after only four weeks?

MA: They told me—the other ChinaMen on the gang. We've been telling stories ever since the strike began.

LONE: They make it sound like it's very enjoyable.

MA: They said it is.

LONE: Oh? And you believe them?

MA: They're my friends. Living underground in winter—sounds exciting, huh?

LONE: Did they say anything about the cold?

MA: Oh, I already know about that. They told me about the mild winters and the warm snow.

LONE: Warm snow?

MA: When I go home, I'll bring some back to show my brothers.

LONE: Bring some—? On the boat?

MA: They'll be shocked—they never seen American snow before.

LONE: You can't. By the time you get snow to the boat, it'll have melted, evaporated, and returned as rain already.

MA: No.

LONE: No?

MA: Stupid.

LONE: Me?

MA: You been here awhile, haven't you?

LONE: Yes. Two years.

MA: Then how come you're so stupid? This is the Gold Mountain. The snow here doesn't melt. It's not wet.

LONE: That's what they told you?

MA: Yeah. It's true.

LONE: Did anyone show you any of this snow?

MA: No. It's not winter.

LONE: So where does it go?

MA: Huh?

LONE: Where does it go, if it doesn't melt? What happens to it?

MA: The snow? I dunno. I guess it just stays around.

LONE: So where is it? Do you see any?

MA: Here? Well, no, but... [*Pause*] This is prob-
    ably one of those places where it doesn't snow—
    even in winter.

LONE: Oh.

MA: Anyway, what's the use of me telling you what
    you already know? Hey, c'mon—teach me some
    of that stuff. Look—I've been practicing the
    walk—how's this? [*Demonstrates*]

LONE: You look like a duck in heat.

MA: Hey—it's a start, isn't it?

LONE: Tell you what—you want to play some *die
    siu*?

MA: *Die siu*? Sure.

LONE: You know, I'm pretty good.

MA: Hey, I play with the guys at camp. You can't
    be any better than Lee—he's really got it down.
    [LONE *pulls out a case with two dice.*]

LONE: I used to play till morning.

MA: Hey, us too. We see the sun start to rise, and
    say, "Hey, if we go to sleep now, we'll never get
    up for work." So we just keep playing.

LONE: [*Holding out dice*] *Die* or *siu*?

MA: *Siu*.

LONE: You sure?

MA: Yeah!

LONE: All right. [*He rolls.*] *Die*!

MA: *Siu*!
    [*They see the result.*]

MA: Not bad.
    [*They continue taking turns rolling through the
    following section;* MA *always loses.*]

LONE: I haven't touched these in two years.

MA: I gotta practice more.

LONE: Have you lost much money?

MA: Huh? So what?

LONE: Oh, you have gold hidden in all your shirt linings, huh?

MA: Here in "America"—losing is no problem. You know—End of the Year Bonus?

LONE: Oh, right.

MA: After I get that, I'll laugh at what I lost.

LONE: Lee told you there was a bonus, right?

MA: How'd you know?

LONE: When I arrived here, Lee told me there was a bonus, too.

MA: Lee teach you how to play?

LONE: Him? He talked to me a lot.

MA: Look, why don't you come down and start playing with the guys again?

LONE: "The guys."

MA: Before we start playing, Lee uses a stick to write "Kill!" in the dirt.

LONE: You seem to live for your nights with "the guys."

MA: What's life without friends, huh?

LONE: Well, why do *you* think I stopped playing?

MA: Hey, maybe you were the one getting killed, huh?

LONE: What?

MA: Hey, just kidding.

LONE: Who's getting killed here?

MA: Just a joke.

LONE: That's not a joke, it's blasphemy.

MA: Look, obviously you stopped playing 'cause you wanted to practice the opera.

LONE: Do you understand that discipline?

MA: But, I mean, you don't have to overdo it either. You don't have to treat 'em like dirt. I mean, who are you trying to impress?

[*Pause.* LONE *throws dice into the bushes.*]

LONE: Oooops. Better go see who won.

MA: Hey! C'mon! Help me look!

LONE: If you find them, they are yours.

MA: You serious?

LONE: Yes.

MA: Here. [*Finds the dice*]

LONE: Who won?

MA: I didn't check.

LONE: Well, no matter. Keep the dice. Take them and go play with your friends.

MA: Here. [*He offers them to* LONE.] A present.

LONE: A present? This isn't a present!

MA: They're mine, aren't they? You gave them to me, right?

LONE: Well, yes, but—

MA: So now I'm giving them to you.

LONE: You can't give me a present. I don't want them.

MA: You wanted them enough to keep them two years.

LONE: I'd forgotten I had them.

MA: See, I know, Lone. You wanna get rid of me. But you can't. I'm paying for lessons.

LONE: With my dice.

MA: Mine now. [*He offers them again.*] Here. [*Pause.* LONE *runs* MA's *hand across his forehead.*]

LONE: Feel this.

MA: Hey!

LONE: Pretty wet, huh?

MA: Big deal.

LONE: Well, it's not from playing *die siu*.

MA: I know how to sweat. I wouldn't be here if I didn't.

LONE: Yes, but are you willing to sweat after you've

finished sweating? Are you willing to come up after you've spent the whole day chipping half an inch off a rock, and punish your body some more?

MA: Yeah. Even after work, I still—

LONE: No, you don't. You want to gamble, and tell dirty stories, and dress up like women to do shows.

MA: Hey, I never did that.

LONE: You've only been here a month. [*Pause*] And what about "the guys"? They're not going to treat you so well once you stop playing with them. Are you willing to work all day listening to them whisper, "That one—let's put spiders in his soup"?

MA: They won't do that to me. With you, it's different.

LONE: Is it?

MA: You don't have to act that way.

LONE: What way?

MA: Like you're so much better than them.

LONE: No. You haven't even begun to understand. To practice every day, you must have a fear to force you up here.

MA: A fear? No—it's 'cause what you're doing is beautiful.

LONE: No.

MA: I've seen it.

LONE: It's ugly to practice when the mountain has turned your muscles to ice. When my body hurts too much to come here, I look at the other ChinaMen and think, "They are dead. Their muscles work only because the white man forces them. I live because I can still force my muscles to work for me." Say it. "They are dead."

MA: No. They're my friends.

LONE: Well, then, take your dice down to your friends.

MA: But I want to learn—

LONE: This is your first lesson.

MA: Look, it shouldn't matter—

LONE: It does.

MA: It shouldn't matter what I think.

LONE: Attitude is everything.

MA: But as long as I come up, do the exercises—

LONE: I'm not going to waste time on a quitter.

MA: I'm not!

LONE: Then say it.—"They are dead men."

MA: I can't.

LONE: Then you will never have the dedication.

MA: That doesn't prove anything.

LONE: I will not teach a dead man.

MA: What?

LONE: If you can't see it, then you're dead too.

MA: Don't start pinning—

LONE: Say it!

MA: All right.

LONE: What?

MA: All right. I'm one of them. I'm a dead man too.

    [*Pause.*]

LONE: I thought as much. So, go. You have your friends.

MA: But I don't have a teacher.

LONE: I don't think you need both.

MA: Are you sure?

LONE: I'm being questioned by a child.

    [LONE *returns to practicing. Silence.*]

MA: Look, Lone, I'll come up here every night— after work—I'll spend my time practicing, okay?

[*Pause*] But I'm not gonna say that they're dead.
Look at them. They're on strike; dead men don't
go on strike, Lone. The white devils—they try
and stick us with a ten-hour day. We want a
return to eight hours and also a fourteen-dollar-
a-month raise. I learned the demon English—
listen: "Eight hour a day good for white man,
alla same good for ChinaMan." These are the
demands of live ChinaMen, Lone. Dead men
don't complain.

LONE: All right, this is something new. But no one
can judge the ChinaMen till after the strike.

MA: They say we'll hold out for months if we have
to. The smart men will live on what we've
hoarded.

LONE: A ChinaMan's mouth can swallow the earth.
[*He takes the dice.*] While the strike is on, I'll
teach you.

MA: And afterwards?

LONE: Afterwards—we'll decide then whether
these are dead or live men.

MA: When can we start?

LONE: We've already begun. Give me your hand.

Scene 3

LONE *and* MA *are doing physical exercises.*

MA: How long will it be before I can play Gwan
Gung?

LONE: How long before a dog can play the violin?

MA: Old Ah Hong—have you heard him play the violin?

LONE: Yes. Now, he should take his violin and give it to a dog.

MA: I think he sounds okay.

LONE: I think he caused that avalanche last winter.

MA: He used to play for weddings back home.

LONE: Ah Hong?

MA: That's what he said.

LONE: You probably heard wrong.

MA: No.

LONE: He probably said he played for funerals.

MA: He's been playing for the guys down at camp.

LONE: He should play for the white devils—that will end this stupid strike.

MA: Yang told me for sure—it'll be over by tomorrow.

LONE: Eight days already. And Yang doesn't know anything.

MA: He said they're already down to an eight-hour day and five dollar raise at the bargaining sessions.

LONE: Yang eats too much opium.

MA: That doesn't mean he's wrong about this.

LONE: You can't trust him. One time—last year— he went around camp looking in everybody's eyes and saying, "Your nails are too long. They're hurting my eyes." This went on for a week. Finally, all the men clipped their nails, made a big pile, which they wrapped in leaves and gave to him. Yang used the nails to season his food—he put it in his soup, sprinkled it on his rice, and never said a word about it again.

Now tell me—are you going to trust a man who eats other men's fingernails?

MA: Well, all I know is we won't go back to work until they meet all our demands. Listen, teach me some Gwan Gung steps.

LONE: I should have expected this. A boy who wants to have twenty wives is the type who demands more than he can handle.

MA: Just a few.

LONE: It takes years before an actor can play Gwan Gung.

MA: I can do it. I spend a lot of time watching the opera when it comes around. Every time I see Gwan Gung, I say, "Yeah. That's me. The god of fighters. The god of adventurers. We have the same kind of spirit."

LONE: I tell you, if you work very hard, when you return to China, you can perhaps be the Second Clown.

MA: Second Clown?

LONE: If you work hard.

MA: What's the Second Clown?

LONE: You can play the *p'i p'a,* and dance and jump all over.

MA: I'll buy them.

LONE: Excuse me?

MA: I'm going to be rich, remember? I'll buy a troupe and force them to let me play Gwan Gung.

LONE: I hope you have enough money, then, to pay audiences to sit through your show.

MA: You mean, I'm going to have to practice here every night—and in return, all I can play is the Second Clown?

LONE: If you work hard.

MA: Am I that bad? Maybe I shouldn't even try to do this. Maybe I should just go down.

LONE: It's not you. Everyone must earn the right to play Gwan Gung. I entered opera school when I was ten years old. My parents decided to sell me for ten years to this opera company. I lived with eighty other boys and we slept in bunks four beds high and hid our candy and rice cakes from each other. After eight years, I was studying to play Gwan Gung.

MA: Eight years?

LONE: I was one of the best in my class. One day, I was summoned by my master, who told me I was to go home for two days, because my mother had fallen very ill and was dying. When I arrived home, Mother was standing at the door waiting, not sick at all. Her first words to me, the son away for eight years, were, "You've been playing while your village has starved. You must go to the Gold Mountain and work."

MA: And you never returned to school?

LONE: I went from a room with eighty boys to a ship with three hundred men. So, you see, it does not come easily to play Gwan Gung.

MA: Did you want to play Gwan Gung?

LONE: What a foolish question!

MA: Well, you're better off this way.

LONE: What?

MA: Actors—they don't make much money. Here, you make a bundle, then go back and be an actor again. Best of both worlds.

LONE: "Best of both worlds."

MA: Yeah!

[LONE *drops to the ground, begins imitating a duck, waddling and quacking.*]

MA: Lone? What are you doing?

[LONE *quacks.*]

You're a duck?

[LONE *quacks.*]

I can see that.

[LONE *quacks.*]

Is this an exercise? Am I supposed to do this?

[LONE *quacks.*]

This is dumb. I never seen Gwan Gung waddle.

[LONE *quacks.*]

Okay. All right. I'll do it.

[MA *and* LONE *quack and waddle.*]

You know, I never realized before how uncomfortable a duck's life is. And you have to listen to yourself quacking all day. Go crazy!

[LONE *stands up straight.*]

Now, what was that all about?

LONE: No, no. Stay down there, duck.

MA: What's the—

LONE: [*Prompting*] Quack, quack, quack.

MA: I don't—

LONE: Act your species!

MA: I'm not a duck!

LONE: Nothing worse than a duck that doesn't know his place.

MA: All right. [*Mechanically*] Quack, quack.

LONE: More.

MA: Quack.

LONE: More!

MA: Quack, quack, quack!

[MA *now continues quacking, as* LONE *gives commands.*]

LONE: Louder! It's your mating call! Think of your
twenty duck wives! Good! Louder! Project! More!
Don't slow down! Put your tail feathers into it!
They can't hear you!

[MA *is now quacking up a storm.* LONE *exits,
unnoticed by* MA.]

MA: Quack! Quack! Quack! Quack. Quack...quack.

[*He looks around.*]

Quack...quack...Lone?...Lone?

[*He waddles around the stage looking.*]

Lone, where are you? Where'd you go?

[*He stops, scratches his left leg with his right
foot.*]

C'mon—stop playing around. What is this?

[LONE *enters as a tiger, unseen by* MA.]

Look, let's call it a day, okay? I'm getting hungry.

[MA *turns around, notices* LONE *right before* LONE
is to bite him.]

Aaaaah! Quack, quack, quack!

[*They face off, in character as animals. Duck-
MA is terrified.*]

LONE: Grrrr!

MA: [*As a cry for help*] Quack, quack, quack!

[LONE *pounces on* MA. *They struggle, in character.* MA *is quacking madly, eyes tightly closed.*
LONE *stands up straight.* MA *continues to quack.*]

LONE: Stand up.

MA: [*Eyes still closed*] Quack, quack, quack!

LONE: [*Louder*] Stand up!

MA: [*Opening his eyes*] Oh.

LONE: What are you?

MA: Huh?

LONE: A ChinaMan or a duck?

MA: Huh? Gimme a second to remember.

LONE: You like being a duck?

MA: My feet fell asleep.

LONE: You change forms so easily.

MA: You said to.

LONE: What else could you turn into?

MA: Well, you scared me—sneaking up like that.

LONE: Perhaps a rock. That would be useful. When the men need to rest, they can sit on you.

MA: I got carried away.

LONE: Let's try...a locust. Can you become a locust?

MA: No. Let's cut this, okay?

LONE: Here. It's easy. You just have to know how to hop.

MA: You're not gonna get me—

LONE: Like this. [*He demonstrates.*]

MA: Forget it, Lone.

LONE: I'm a locust. [*He begins jumping toward* MA.]

MA: Hey! Get away!

LONE: I devour whole fields.

MA: Stop it.

LONE: I starve babies before they are born.

MA: Hey, look, stop it!

LONE: I cause famines and destroy villages.

MA: I'm warning you! Get away!

LONE: What are you going to do? You can't kill a locust.

MA: You're not a locust.

LONE: You kill one, and another sits on your hand.

MA: Stop following me.

LONE: Locusts always trouble people. If not, we'd feel useless. Now, if you became a locust, too...

MA: I'm not going to become a locust.

LONE: Just stick your teeth out!

MA: I'm not gonna be a bug! It's stupid!

LONE: No man who's just been a duck has the right to call anything stupid.

MA: I thought you were trying to teach me something.

LONE: I am. Go ahead.

MA: All right. There. That look right?

LONE: Your legs should be a little lower. Lower! There. That's adequate. So, how does it feel to be a locust? [LONE *gets up.*]

MA: I dunno. How long do I have to do this?

LONE: Could you do it for three years?

MA: Three years? Don't be—

LONE: You couldn't, could you? Could you be a duck for that long?

MA: Look, I wasn't born to be either of those.

LONE: Exactly. Well, I wasn't born to work on a railroad, either. "Best of both worlds." How can you be such an insect!

[*Pause.*]

MA: Lone...

LONE: Stay down there! Don't move! I've never told anyone my story—the story of my parents' kidnapping me from school. All the time we were crossing the ocean, the last two years here— I've kept my mouth shut. To you, I finally tell it. And all you can say is, "Best of both worlds." You're a bug to me, a locust. You think you understand the dedication one must have to be in the opera? You think it's the same as working on a railroad.

MA: Lone, all I was saying is that you'll go back too, and—

LONE: You're no longer a student of mine.

MA: What?

LONE: You have no dedication.

MA: Lone, I'm sorry.

LONE: Get up.

MA: I'm honored that you told me that.

LONE: Get up.

MA: No.

LONE: No?

MA: I don't want to. I want to talk.

LONE: Well, I've learned from the past. You're stubborn. You don't go. All right. Stay there. If you want to prove to me that you're dedicated, be a locust till morning. I'll go.

MA: Lone, I'm really honored that you told me.

LONE: I'll return in the morning. [*Exits.*]

MA: Lone? Lone, that's ridiculous. You think I'm gonna stay like this? If you do, you're crazy. Lone? Come back here.

Scene 4

Night. MA, *alone, as a locust.*

MA: Locusts travel in huge swarms, so large that when they cross the sky, they block out the sun, like a storm. Second Uncle—back home—when he was a young man, his whole crop got wiped out by locusts one year. In the famine that followed, Second Uncle lost his eldest son and his second wife—the one he married for love. Even to this day, we look around before saying the word "locust," to make sure Second Uncle is out

of hearing range. About eight years ago, my
brother and I discovered Second Uncle's cave
in back of the stream near our house. We saw
him come out of it one day around noon. Later,
just before the sun went down, we sneaked in.
We only looked once. Inside, there must have
been hundreds—maybe five hundred or more—
grasshoppers in huge bamboo cages—and
around them—stacks of grasshopper legs,
grasshopper heads, grasshopper antennae,
grasshoppers with one leg, still trying to hop
but toppling like trees coughing, grasshoppers
wrapped around sharp branches rolling from
side to side, grasshopper legs cut off grasshopper bodies, then tied around grasshoppers and
tightened till grasshoppers died. Every conceivable kind of grasshopper in every conceivable stage of life and death, subject to every
conceivable grasshopper torture. We ran out
quickly, my brother and I—we knew an evil
place by the thickness of the air. Now, I think
of Second Uncle. How sad that the locusts forced
him to take out his agony on innocent grasshoppers. What if Second Uncle could see me
now? Would he cut off my legs? He might as
well. I can barely feel them. But then again,
Second Uncle never tortured actual locusts, just
weak grasshoppers.

Scene 5

Night. MA *still as a locust.*

LONE: [*Off, singing.*]

> Hit your hardest
> Pound out your tears
> The more you try
> The more you'll cry
> At how little I've moved
> And how large I loom
> By the time the sun goes down

MA: You look rested.
LONE: Me?
MA: Well, you sound rested.
LONE: No, not at all.
MA: Maybe I'm just comparing you to me.
LONE: I didn't even close my eyes all last night.
MA: Aw, Lone, you didn't have to stay up for me.
    You coulda just come up here and—
LONE: For you?
MA: —apologized and everything woulda been—
LONE: I didn't stay up for you.
MA: Huh? You didn't?
LONE: No.
MA: Oh. You sure?
LONE: Positive. I was thinking, that's all.
MA: About me?

85

LONE: Well...

MA: Even a little?

LONE: I was thinking about the ChinaMen—and you. Get up, Ma.

MA: Aw, do I have to? I've gotten to know these grasshoppers real well.

LONE: Get up. I have a lot to tell you.

MA: What'll they think? They take me in, even though I'm a little large, then they find out I'm a human being. I stepped on their kids. No trust. Gimme a hand, will you? [LONE *helps* MA *up, but* MA's *legs can't support him.*] Aw, shit. My legs are coming off. [*He lies down and tries to straighten them out.*]

LONE: I have many surprises. First, you will play Gwan Gung.

MA: My legs will be sent home without me. What'll my family think? Come to port to meet me and all they get is two legs.

LONE: Did you hear me?

MA: Hold on. I can't be in agony and listen to Chinese at the same time.

LONE: Did you hear my first surprise?

MA: No. I'm too busy screaming.

LONE: I said, you'll play Gwan Gung.

MA: Gwan Gung?

LONE: Yes.

MA: Me?

LONE: Yes.

MA: Without legs?

LONE: What?

MA: That might be good.

LONE: Stop that!

MA: I'll become a legend. Like the blind man who defended Amoy.

LONE: Did you hear?

MA: "The legless man who played Gwan Gung."

LONE: Isn't this what you want? To play Gwan Gung?

MA: No, I just wanna sleep.

LONE: No, you don't. Look. Here. I brought you something.

MA: Food?

LONE: Here. Some rice.

MA: Thanks, Lone. And duck?

LONE: Just a little.

MA: Where'd you get the duck?

LONE: Just bones and skin.

MA: We don't have duck. And the white devils have been blockading the food.

LONE: Sing—he had some left over.

MA: Sing? That thief?

LONE: And something to go with it.

MA: What? Lone, where did you find whiskey?

LONE: You know, Sing—he has almost anything.

MA: Yeah. For a price.

LONE: Once, even some thousand-day-old eggs.

MA: He's a thief. That's what they told me.

LONE: Not if you're his friend.

MA: Sing don't have any real friends. Everyone talks about him bein' tied in to the head of the klan in San Francisco. Lone, you didn't have to do this. Here. Have some.

LONE: I had plenty.

MA: Don't gimme that. This cost you plenty, Lone.

LONE: Well, I thought if we were going to celebrate, we should do it as well as we would at home.

MA: Celebrate? What for? Wait.

LONE: Ma, the strike is over.

MA: Shit, I knew it. And we won, right?

LONE: Yes, the ChinaMen have won. They can do more than just talk.

MA: I told you. Didn't I tell you?

LONE: Yes. Yes, you did.

MA: Yang told me it was gonna be done. He said—

LONE: Yes, I remember.

MA: Didn't I tell you? Huh?

LONE: Ma, eat your duck.

MA: Nine days. In nine days, we civilized the white devils. I knew it. I knew we'd hold out till their ears started twitching. So that's where you got the duck, right? At the celebration?

LONE: No, there wasn't a celebration.

MA: Huh? You sure? ChinaMen—they look for any excuse to party.

LONE: But I thought *we* should celebrate.

MA: Well, that's for sure.

LONE: So you will play Gwan Gung.

MA: God, nine days. Shit, it's finally done. Well, we'll show them how to party. Make noise. Jump off rocks. Make the mountain shake.

LONE: We'll wash your body, to prepare you for the role.

MA: What role?

LONE: Gwan Gung. I've been telling you.

MA: I don't wanna play Gwan Gung.

LONE: You've shown the dedication required to become my student, so—

MA: Lone, you think I stayed up last night 'cause I wanted to play Gwan Gung?

LONE: You said you were like him.

MA: I am. Gwan Gung stayed up all night once to prove his loyalty. Well, now I have too. Lone, I'm honored that you told me your story.

LONE: Yes...That is like Gwan Gung.

MA: Good. So let's do an opera about *me*.

LONE: What?

MA: You wanna party or what?

LONE: About you?

MA: You said I was like Gwan Gung, didn't you?

LONE: Yes, but—

MA: Well, look at the operas he's got. I ain't even got one.

LONE: Still, you can't—

MA: You tell me, is that fair?

LONE: You can't do an opera about yourself.

MA: I just won a victory, didn't I? I deserve an opera in my honor.

LONE: But it's not traditional.

MA: Traditional? Lone, you gotta figure any way I could do Gwan Gung wasn't gonna be traditional anyway. I may be as good a guy as him, but he's a better dancer. [*Sings*]

Old Gwan Gung, just sits about
Till the dime-store fighters have had it out
Then he pitches his peach pit
Combs his beard
Draws his sword
And they scatter in fear

LONE: What are you talking about?

MA: I just won a great victory. I get—whatcha call it?—poetic license. C'mon. Hit the gongs. I'll immortalize my story.

LONE: I refuse. This goes against all my training. I try and give you your wish and—

MA: Do it. Gimme my wish. Hit the gongs.

LONE: I never—I can't.

MA: Can't what? Don't think I'm worth an opera?
No, I guess not. I forgot—you think I'm just
one of those dead men.
[*Silence.* LONE *pulls out a gong.* MA *gets into
position.* LONE *hits the gong. They do the following in a mock-Chinese-opera style.*]

MA: I am Ma. Yesterday, I was kicked out of my
house by my three elder brothers, calling me
the lazy dreamer of the family. I am sitting here
in front of the temple trying to decide how I
will avenge this indignity. Here comes the poor-
est beggar in this village. [*He cues* LONE.] He
is called Fleaman because his body is the most
popular meeting place for fleas from around the
province.

LONE: [*Singing*]

> Fleas in love,
> Find your happiness
> In the gray scraps of my suit

MA: Hello, Flea—
LONE: [*Continuing*]

> Fleas in need,
> Shield your families
> In the gray hairs of my beard

MA: Hello, Flea—
[LONE *cuts* MA *off, continues an extended im-
provised aria.*]
MA: Hello, Fleaman.
LONE: Hello, Ma. Are you interested in providing
a home for these fleas?

MA: No!

LONE: This couple here—seeking to start a new home. Housing today is so hard to find. How about your left arm?

MA: I may have plenty of my own fleas in time. I have been thrown out by my elder brothers.

LONE: Are you seeking revenge? A flea epidemic on your house? [*To a flea*] Get back there. You should be asleep. Your mother will worry.

MA: Nothing would make my brothers angrier than seeing me rich.

LONE: Rich? After the bad crops of the last three years, even the fleas are thinking of moving north.

MA: I heard a white devil talk yesterday.

LONE: Oh—with hair the color of a sick chicken and eyes round as eggs? The fleas and I call him Chicken-Laying-an-Egg.

MA: He said we can make our fortunes on the Gold Mountain, where work is play and the sun scares off snow.

LONE: Don't listen to chicken-brains.

MA: Why not? He said gold grows like weeds.

LONE: I have heard that it is slavery.

MA: Slavery? What do you know, Fleaman? Who told you? The fleas? Yes, I will go to Gold Mountain.

[*Gongs.* MA *strikes a submissive pose to* LONE.]

LONE: "The one hundred twenty-five dollars passage money is to be paid to the said head of said Hong, who will make arrangements with the coolies, that their wages shall be deducted until the debt is absorbed."

[MA *bows to* LONE. *Gongs. They pick up fighting*

*sticks and do a water-crossing dance. Dance
ends. They stoop next to each other and rock.*]

MA: I have been in the bottom of this boat for thirty-
six days now. Tang, how many have died?

LONE: Not me. I'll live through this ride.

MA: I didn't ask how you are.

LONE: But why's the Gold Mountain so far?

MA: We left with three hundred and three.

LONE: My family's depending on me.

MA: So tell me, how many have died?

LONE: I'll be the last one alive.

MA: That's not what I wanted to know.

LONE: I'll find some fresh air in this hole.

MA: I asked, how many have died.

LONE: Is that a crack in the side?

MA: Are you listening to me?

LONE: If I had some air —

MA: I asked, don't you see —?

LONE: The crack — over there —

MA: Will you answer me, please?

LONE: I need to get out.

MA: The rest here agree —

LONE: I can't stand the smell.

MA: That a hundred eighty —

LONE: I can't see the air —

MA: Of us will not see —

LONE: And I can't die.

MA: Our Gold Mountain dream.

[LONE/TANG *dies;* MA *throws his body overboard.
The boat docks.* MA *exits, walks through the
streets. He picks up one of the fighting sticks,
while* LONE *becomes the mountain.*]

MA: I have been given my pickax. Now I will at-
tack the mountain.

[MA *does a dance of labor.* LONE *sings.*]
LONE:

> Hit your hardest
> Pound out your tears
> The more you try
> The more you'll cry
> At how little I've moved
> And how large I loom
> By the time the sun goes down

[*Dance stops.*]

MA: This mountain is clever. But why shouldn't it be? It's fighting for its life, like we fight for ours.

[*The* MOUNTAIN *picks up a stick.* MA *and the* MOUNTAIN *do a battle dance. Dance ends.*]

MA: This mountain not only defends itself—it also attacks. It turns our strength against us.

[LONE *does* MA's *labor dance, while* MA *plants explosives in midair. Dance ends.*]

MA: This mountain has survived for millions of years. Its wisdom is immense.

[LONE *and* MA *begin a second battle dance. This one ends with them working the battle sticks together.* LONE *breaks away, does a warrior strut.*]

LONE: I am a white devil! Listen to my stupid language: "Wha che doo doo blah blah." Look at my wide eyes—like I have drunk seventy-two pots of tea. Look at my funny hair—twisting, turning, like a snake telling lies. [*To* MA] Bla bla doo doo tee tee.

MA: We don't understand English.

LONE: [*Angry*] Bla bla doo doo tee tee!

MA: [*With Chinese accent*] Please you-ah speak-ah Chinese?

LONE: Oh.   Work—uh—one—two—more—work—two—

MA: Two hours more? Stupid demons. As confused as your hair. We will strike!

[*Gongs.* MA *is on strike.*]

MA: [*In broken English*] Eight hours day good for white man, alla same good for ChinaMan.

LONE: The strike is over! We've won!

MA: I knew we would.

LONE: We forced the white devil to act civilized.

MA: Tamed the barbarians!

LONE: Did you think—

MA: Who woulda thought?

LONE: —it could be done?

MA: Who?

LONE: But who?

MA: Who could tame them?

MA *and* LONE: Only a ChinaMan! [*They laugh.*]

LONE: Well, c'mon.

MA: Let's celebrate!

LONE: We have.

MA: Oh.

LONE: Back to work.

MA: But we've won the strike.

LONE: I know. Congratulations! And now—

MA: —back to work?

LONE: Right.

MA: No.

LONE: But the strike is over.

[LONE *tosses* MA *a stick. They resume their stick battle as before, but* MA *is heard over* LONE'S *singing.*]

LONE:
Hit your hardest
Pound out your
  tears
The more you try
The more you'll cry
At how little I've
  moved
And how large I
  loom
By the time the
  sun goes down.

MA:
Wait.
I'm tired of this!
How do we end it?
Let's stop now, all
  right?
Look, I said enough!

[MA *tosses his stick away, but* LONE *is already aiming a blow toward it, so that* LONE *hits* MA *instead and knocks him down.*]

MA: Oh! Shit...
LONE: I'm sorry! Are you all right?
MA: Yeah. I guess.
LONE: Why'd you let go? You can't just do that.
MA: I'm bleeding.
LONE: That was stupid—where?
MA: Here.
LONE: No.
MA: Ow!
LONE: There will probably be a bump.
MA: I dunno.
LONE: What?
MA: I dunno why I let go.
LONE: It was stupid.
MA: But how were we going to end the opera?
LONE: Here. [*He applies whiskey to* MA's *bruise.*] I don't know.
MA: Why didn't we just end it with the celebration? Ow! Careful.

LONE: Sorry. But Ma, the celebration's not the end. We're returning to work. Today. At dawn.

MA: What?

LONE: We've already lost nine days of work. But we got eight hours.

MA: Today? That's terrible.

LONE: What do you think we're here for? But they listened to our demands. We're getting a raise.

MA: Right. Fourteen dollars.

LONE: No. Eight.

MA: What?

LONE: We had to compromise. We got an eight-dollar raise.

MA: But we wanted fourteen. Why didn't we get fourteen?

LONE: It was the best deal they could get. Congratulations.

MA: Congratulations? Look, Lone, I'm sick of you making fun of the ChinaMen.

LONE: Ma, I'm not. For the first time. I was wrong. We got eight dollars.

MA: We wanted fourteen.

LONE: But we got eight hours.

MA: We'll go back on strike.

LONE: Why?

MA: We could hold out for months.

LONE: And lose all that work?

MA: But we just gave in.

LONE: You're being ridiculous. We got eight hours. Besides, it's already been decided.

MA: I didn't decide. I wasn't there. You made me stay up here.

LONE: The heads of the gangs decide.

MA: And that's it?

LONE: It's done.

MA: Back to work? That's what they decided? Lone, I don't want to go back to work.

LONE: Who does?

MA: I forgot what it's like.

LONE: You'll pick up the technique again soon enough.

MA: I mean, what it's like to have them telling you what to do all the time. Using up your strength.

LONE: I thought you said even after work, you still feel good.

MA: Some days. But others... [*Pause*] I get so frustrated sometimes. At the rock. The rock doesn't give in. It's not human. I wanna claw it with my fingers, but that would just rip them up. I wanna throw myself head first onto it, but it'd just knock my skull open. The rock would knock my skull open, then just sit there, still, like nothing had happened, like a faceless Buddha. [*Pause*] Lone, when do I get out of here?

LONE: Well, the railroad may get finished—

MA: It'll never get finished.

LONE: —or you may get rich.

MA: Rich. Right. This is the Gold Mountain. [*Pause*] Lone, has anyone ever gone home rich from here?

LONE: Yes. Some.

MA: But most?

LONE: Most... do go home.

MA: Do you still have the fear?

LONE: The fear?

MA: That you'll become like them—dead men?

LONE: Maybe I was wrong about them.

MA: Well, I do. You wanted me to say it before. I

can say it now: "They are dead men." Their greatest accomplishment was to win a strike that's gotten us nothing.

LONE: They're sending money home.

MA: No.

LONE: It's not much, I know, but it's something.

MA: Lone, I'm not even doing that. If I don't get rich here, I might as well die here. Let my brothers laugh in peace.

LONE: Ma, you're too soft to get rich here, naïve— you believed the snow was warm.

MA: I've got to change myself. Toughen up. Take no shit. Count my change. Learn to gamble. Learn to win. Learn to stare. Learn to deny. Learn to look at men with opaque eyes.

LONE: You want to do that?

MA: I will. 'Cause I've got the fear. You've given it to me.

[*Pause.*]

LONE: Will I see you here tonight?

MA: Tonight?

LONE: I just thought I'd ask.

MA: I'm sorry, Lone. I haven't got time to be the Second Clown.

LONE: I thought you might not.

MA: Sorry.

LONE: You could have been a... fair actor.

MA: You coming down? I gotta get ready for work. This is gonna be a terrible day. My legs are sore and my arms are outa practice.

LONE: You go first. I'm going to practice some before work. There's still time.

MA: Practice? But you said you lost your fear. And you said that's what brings you up here.

LONE: I guess I was wrong about that, too. Today,

I am dancing for no reason at all.

MA: Do whatever you want. See you down at camp.

LONE: Could you do me a favor?

MA: A favor?

LONE: Could you take this down so I don't have to take it all?

[LONE *points to a pile of props*.]

MA: Well, okay. [*Pause*] But this is the last time.

LONE: Of course, Ma. [MA *exits*.] See you soon. The last time. I suppose so.

[LONE *resumes practicing. He twirls his hair around as in the beginning of the play. The sun begins to rise. It continues rising until* LONE *is moving and seen only in shadow*.]

CURTAIN

FAMILY DEVOTIONS

*For my Ama and Ankong,
and Sam Shepard*

Family Devotions was produced by Joseph Papp at the New York Shakespeare Festival Public Theater, where it opened in the Newman Theater on October 18, 1981, with the following cast:

JOANNE	Jodi Long
WILBUR	Jim Ishida
JENNY	Lauren Tom
AMA	Tina Chen
POPO	June Kim
HANNAH	Helen Funai
ROBERT	Michael Paul Chan
DI-GOU	Victor Wong
CHESTER	Marc Hayashi

Directed by Robert Alan Ackerman. Settings by David Gropman. Lights by Tom Skelton. Costumes by Willa Kim.

CHARACTERS

JOANNE, late thirties, Chinese American raised in the Philippines.

WILBUR, her husband, Japanese American, nisei (second generation).

JENNY, their daughter, seventeen.

AMA, Joanne's mother, born in China, emigrated to the Philippines, then to America.

POPO, Ama's younger sister.

HANNAH, Popo's daughter and Joanne's cousin, slightly older than Joanne.

ROBERT, Hannah's husband, Chinese American, first generation.

DI-GOU, Ama and Popo's younger brother, born and raised in China, still a resident of the People's Republic of China (P.R.C.).

CHESTER, Hannah and Robert's son, early twenties.

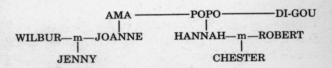

103

David Henry Hwang

SYNOPSIS OF SCENES

ACT I. Late afternoon, the lanai/sunroom and tennis court of a home in Bel Air, California.
ACT II. Same scene, immediately following.

DEFINITION

Jok is a Chinese rice porridge.

ACT I

The sunroom and backyard of a home in Bel Air. Everywhere is glass—glass roof, glass walls. Upstage of the lanai/sunroom is a patio with a barbecue and a tennis court. The tennis court leads offstage. As the curtain rises, we see a single spotlight on an old Chinese face and hear Chinese music or chanting. Suddenly, the music becomes modern-day funk or rock 'n' roll, and the lights come up to reveal the set.

The face is that of DI-GOU, *an older Chinese man wearing a blue suit and carrying an old suitcase. He is peering into the sunroom from the tennis court, through the glass walls. Behind him, a stream of black smoke is coming from the barbecue.*

[*Offstage*] Wilbur! Wilbur!
> [DI-GOU *exits off the tennis court. Enter* JOANNE, *from the house. She is a Chinese American woman, attractive, in her mid-thirties. She sees the smoke coming from the barbecue.*]

JOANNE: Aiii-ya! [*She heads for the barbecue, and on her way notices that the sunroom is a mess.*] Jenny! [*She runs out to the barbecue, opens it*

up. Billows of black smoke continue to pour out.]
Oh, gosh. Oh, golly. [*To offstage*] Wilbur! [*She
begins pulling burnt objects out of the barbecue.*]
Sheee! [*She pulls out a chicken, dumps it onto
the ground.*] Wilbur! [*She pulls out another
chicken, does the same.]* Wilbur, the heat was
too high on the barbecue! [*She begins pulling
out burnt objects and tossing them all over the
tennis court.*] You should have been watching
it! It could have exploded! We could all have
been blown up! [*She picks up another chicken,
examines it.*] You think we can have some of
this? [*She pauses, tosses it onto the court.*] We'll
get some more chickens. We'll put barbecue
sauce on them and stick them into the microwave. [*She exits into the house holding a chicken
on the end of her fork.]* Is this okay, do you
think?
[WILBUR *appears on the tennis court. He is a
Japanese American man, nisei, in his late thirties. His hair is permed. He wears tennis clothes.*]
WILBUR: Hon? [*He looks around.*] What's up? [*He
picks a burnt chicken off the tennis court.]* Hon?
[*He walks over to the barbecue.*] Who—? Why's
the heat off? [*He walks around the tennis court
picking up chickens.*] Jesus! [*He smears grease
on his white tennis shirt, notices it.*] Aw, shit!
[*He dumps all the chickens except one, which he
has forgotten to pick up, back into the barbecue.
He walks into the sunroom, gets some ice, and
tries to dab at the stain.*] Hon? Will you come
here a sec? [*He exits into the house.*]
[JENNY *appears on the tennis court. She is seventeen,* WILBUR *and* JOANNE's *daughter. She*

carries a large wire-mesh box.]

JENNY: Chickie! [Looking around] Chickie? Chickie, where the hell did you go? You know, it's embarrassing. It's embarrassing being this old and still having to chase a chicken all over the house. [She sees the lone burnt chicken on the court. She creeps over slowly, then picks it up.] Blaagh! Who cooked this? See, Chickie, this is what happens—what happens when you're a bad chickie.

[CHESTER, a young Chinese American male in his early twenties, appears on the tennis court. He tries to sneak up on JENNY.]

JENNY: [To chicken] Look, if you bother Popo and Ama, I'm gonna catch shit, and you know what that means for you—chicken soccer. You'll be sorry. [CHESTER is right behind JENNY.] You'll be sorry if you mess with me. [She turns around, catching CHESTER.] Oh, good. You have to be here, too.

CHESTER: No, I don't. I've gotta pack.

JENNY: They'll expect you to be here when that Chinese guy gets here. What's his name? Dargwo?

CHESTER: I dunno. Dah-gim?

JENNY: Doo-goo? Something.

CHESTER: Yeah. I'm not staying.

JENNY: So what else is new?

CHESTER: I don't have time.

JENNY: You luck out 'cause you don't live here. Me—there's no way I can get away. When you leaving?

CHESTER: Tomorrow.

JENNY: Tomorrow? And you're not packed?

CHESTER: Don't rub it in. Listen, you still have my green suitcase?

JENNY: Yeah. I wish *I* had an excuse not to be here. All I need is to meet another old relative. Another goon.

CHESTER: Yeah. Where's my suitcase?

JENNY: First you have to help me find Chickie.

CHESTER: Jesus!

AMA: [*Offstage*] Joanne!

CHESTER: [*To* JENNY] All right. I don't want them to know I'm here.

[CHESTER *and* JENNY *exit.* POPO *and* AMA *enter. They are* JOANNE's *aunt and mother, respectively.*]

AMA: Joanne! Joanne! Jenny! Where is Joanne?

POPO: Probably busy.

AMA: Where is Jenny? Joanne?

POPO: Perhaps you can find, ah, Wilbur.

AMA: Joanne!

POPO: Ah, you never wish to see Wilbur.

AMA: I see him at wedding. That is enough. He was not at church again today.

POPO: Ah?

AMA: He will be bad influence when Di-gou arrive. Wilbur—holy spirit is not in him.

POPO: Not matter. He can perhaps eat in kitchen.

AMA: Outside!

POPO: This is his house.

AMA: All heart must join as one—

POPO: He may eat inside!

AMA: —only then, miracles can take place.

POPO: But in kitchen.

AMA: Wilbur—he never like family devotions.

POPO: Wilbur does not come from Christian family.

AMA: He come from Japanese family.

POPO: I mean to say, we—ah—very fortunate. Mama teach us all Christianity. Not like Wilbur family.

AMA: When Di-gou arrive, we will remind him. What Mama tells us.

POPO: Di-gou can remember himself.

AMA: No.

POPO: But we remember.

AMA: You forget—Di-gou, he lives in China.

POPO: So?

AMA: Torture. Communists. Make him work in rice fields.

POPO: I no longer think so.

AMA: In rice field, all the people wear wires in their heads—yes! Wires force them work all day and sing Communist song. Like this! [*She mimes harvesting rice and singing.*]

POPO: No such thing!

AMA: Yes! You remember Twa-Ling? Before we leave China, before Communist come, she say, "I will send you a picture. If Communists are good, I will stand—if bad, I will sit."

POPO: That does not mean anything!

AMA: In picture she sent, she was lying down!

POPO: Picture was not sent for ten years. Probably she forget.

AMA: You wait till Di-gou arrive. You will see.

POPO: See what?

AMA: Brainwash! You watch for little bit of wires in his hair. [POPO *notices the lone burnt chicken on the tennis court.*]

POPO: What's there?

AMA: Where?

POPO: There—on cement.

AMA: Cannot see well.

POPO: There. Black.

AMA: Oh. I see.

POPO: Looks like *gao sai*.

AMA: They sometimes have problem with the dog.

POPO: Ha!

AMA: Very bad dog.

POPO: At home, dog do that?—we shoot him.

AMA: Should be punish.

POPO: Shot! [*Pause*] That no *gao sai*.

AMA: No? What then?

POPO: I don't know.

AMA: Oh, I know.

POPO: What?

AMA: That is Chickie.

POPO: No. That no Chickie.

AMA: They have a chicken—"Chickie."
   [*They get up, head toward the chicken.*]

POPO: No. That one, does not move.

AMA: Maybe sick. [*They reach the chicken.*] Aiii-
   ya! What happen to Chickie!

POPO: [*Picking it up*] This chicken very sick! [*She
   laughs.*]

AMA: Wilbur.

POPO: Huh?

AMA: Wilbur—his temper is very bad.

POPO: No!

AMA: Yes. Perhaps Chickie bother him too much.

POPO: No—this is only a chicken.

AMA: "Chickie" *is* chicken!

POPO: No—this—another chicken.

AMA: How you know?

POPO: No matter now. Like this, all chicken look

same. Here. Throw away. No good.

AMA: Very bad temper. Japanese man. [AMA *sees* POPO *looking for a trash can.*] Wait.

POPO: Huh?

AMA: Jenny—might want to keep it.

POPO: This?

AMA: Leave here until we know. [*She takes the chicken from* POPO.]

POPO: No, throw away. [*She takes it back.*] Stink up whole place soon.

AMA: Don't want to anger Wilbur!

POPO: You pig-head!

AMA: He do this to Chickie—think what he will do to us?

POPO: *Zin gao tza!* [Always so much trouble!]

AMA: You don't know Japanese man!
  [AMA *knocks the chicken from* POPO's *hands; they circle around it like boxers sparring.*]

POPO: *Pah-di!* [Spank you!]

AMA: Remember? During war? Pictures they show us? Always—Japanese man kill Chinese!

POPO: Go away, pig-head!

AMA: In picture—Japanese always kill and laugh, kill and laugh.

POPO: If dirty, should throw away!

AMA: Sometimes—torture and laugh, too.

POPO: Wilbur not like that! Hardly even laugh!

AMA: When he kill Chickie, then he laugh!
  [*They both grab the chicken;* JOANNE *enters, sees them.*]

JOANNE: Hi, Mom, Auntie. Who cleaned up the chicken?

AMA: Huh? This is not Chickie?

POPO: [*To* AMA] Tell you things, you never listen.

Gong-gong-ah! [Idiot!]

JOANNE: When's Hannah getting here?

POPO: Hannah—she is at airport.

JOANNE: We had a little accident and I need help programming the microwave. Last time, I put a roast inside and it disintegrated. She should be here already.

AMA: Joanne, you prepare for family devotions?

JOANNE: Of course, Mom. I had the maid set up everything just like you said.
[*She exits.*]

AMA: Good. Praise to God will bring Di-gou back to family. Make him rid of Communist demon.

POPO: He will speak in tongue of fire. Like he does when he is a little boy with See-goh-poh.
[WILBUR *enters the tennis court with an empty laundry basket. He heads for the barbecue.* JOANNE *follows him.*]

JOANNE: [*To* WILBUR] Hon, what are you going to do with those?

WILBUR: [*Referring to the burnt chicken*] I'm just going to give them to Grizzly. [*He piles the chickens into the basket.*]

JOANNE: All right. [*She notices that the mess in the lanai has not been touched.*] Jenny! [*To* WILBUR] But be careful not to give Grizzly any bones!
[JOANNE *exits.*]

WILBUR: [*To* AMA *and* POPO] How you doin', Mom, Auntie?

AMA: [*To* POPO, *sotto voce*] Kill and laugh.

WILBUR: Joanne tells me you're pretty excited about your brother's arrival—pretty understandable, after all these years—what's his name again? Di-ger, Di-gow, something...

AMA: Di-gou!

WILBUR: Yeah, right. Gotta remember that. Be
pretty embarrassing if I said the wrong name.
Di-gou.

POPO: Di-gou is not his name.

WILBUR: What? Not his—? What is it again? Di-gow?
De—?

AMA: Di-gou!

WILBUR: Di-gou.

POPO: That is not his name.

WILBUR: Oh. It's the tones in Chinese, isn't it? I'm
saying the wrong tone: Di-gou? Or Di-gou? Or—

POPO: Di-gou meaning is "second brother."

WILBUR: Oh, I see. It's not his name. Boy, do I feel
ignorant in these situations. If only there were
some way I could make sure I don't embarrass
myself tonight.

AMA: Eat outside.

WILBUR: Outside?

POPO: Or in kitchen.

WILBUR: In the kitchen? That's great! You two are
real jokers, you know?

AMA: No. We are not.

WILBUR: C'mon. I should bring you down to the
club someday. The guys never believe it when
I tell them how much I love you two.

AMA: [To POPO] Gao sai.

[JENNY enters the sunroom.]

WILBUR: Right. "Gao sai" to you, too. [He starts to
leave, sees JENNY.] Wash your hands before you
play with your grandmother.

JENNY: [To WILBUR] Okay, Dad. [To AMA] Do I
have to, Ama?

AMA: No. Of course not.

JENNY: Can I ask you something personal?

AMA: Of course.

JENNY: Did Daddy just call you "dog shit"?

AMA: Jenny!

POPO: Yes. Very good!

JENNY: Doesn't that bother you?

POPO: [*To* AMA] Her Chinese is improving!

JENNY: We learned it in Chinese school.

AMA: Jenny, you should not use this American word.

JENNY: Sorry. It just slipped out.

AMA: You do not use such word at school, no?

JENNY: Oh, no. Of course not.

AMA: You should not use anyplace.

JENNY: Right.

POPO: Otherwise—no good man wants marry you.

JENNY: You mean, no rich man.

AMA: No—money is not important.

POPO: As long as he is good man.
    [*Pause.*]

AMA: Christian.

POPO: Chinese.

AMA: Good education.

POPO: Good school.

AMA: Princeton.

POPO: Harvard.

AMA: Doctor.

POPO: Surgeon.

AMA: Brain surgeon.

POPO: Surgeon general.

AMA: Otherwise—you marry anyone that you like.

JENNY: Ama, Popo—look, I'm only seventeen.

POPO: True. But you can develop the good habits now.

JENNY: I don't want to get married till I'm at least thirty or something.

POPO: Thirty! By that time we are dead!

AMA: Gone to see God!

POPO: Lie in ground, arms cross!

JENNY: Look at it this way: how can I be a good mother if I have to follow my career around?

AMA: Your career will not require this.

JENNY: Yeah, it will. What if I have to go on tour?

AMA: Dental technicians do not tour.

JENNY: Ama!

POPO: Only tour—one mouth to next mouth: "Hello. Clean your teeth?"

JENNY: Look, I'm telling you, I'm going to be a dancer.

AMA: We say—you can do both. Combine skills.

JENNY: That's ridiculous.

POPO: Be first dancing dental technician.

JENNY: I don't wanna be a dental technician!

POPO: Dancing dental technician very rare. You will be very popular.

JENNY: Why can't I be like Chester?

AMA: You cannot be like Chester.

JENNY: Why not!

POPO: You do not play violin. Chester does not dance. No hope.

JENNY: I know, but, I mean, he's a musician. Why can't I be a dancer?

AMA: Chester—his work very dangerous.

JENNY: Dangerous?

AMA: He just receive new job—play with Boston Symphony.

JENNY: Yeah. I know. He's leaving tomorrow. So? What's so bad about Boston?

AMA: Conductor—Ozawa—he is Japanese.

JENNY: Oh, no. Not this again.

AMA: Very strict. If musicians miss one note, they must kill themself!

JENNY: Don't be ridiculous. That's no reason why I can't be like Chester.

POPO: But Chester—he makes plenty money.

JENNY: Yeah. Right. Now. But he has to leave home to do it, see? I want a career, too. So what if I never get married?

AMA: Jenny! You must remember—you come from family of See-goh-poh. She was a great evangelist.

JENNY: I know about See-goh-poh. She was your aunt.

AMA: First in family to become Christian.

POPO: She make this family chosen by God.

JENNY: To do what? Clean teeth?

AMA: Jenny!

JENNY: Look, See-goh-poh never got married because of her work, right?

AMA: See-goh-poh was marry to God.

POPO: When Di-gou arrive, he will tell you his testimony. How See-goh-poh change his life.

AMA: Before, he is like you. [*To* POPO] You remember?

POPO: Yes. He is always so fussy.

JENNY: I'm not fussy.

AMA: Stubborn.

POPO: Complain this, complain that.

JENNY: I'm not complaining!

AMA: He will be very happy to meet you. Someone to complain with.

JENNY: I'm just telling you, there's no such thing as a dancing dental technician!

AMA: Good. You will be new discovery.

POPO: When Di-gou is a little boy, he never play
with other children. He only read the books.
Read books—and play tricks.

AMA: He is very naughty.

POPO: He tell other children there are ghosts hide
inside the tree, behind the bush, in the bathroom at night.

AMA: One day, he feed snail poison to gardener.

POPO: Then, when he turns eight year old, See-
goh-poh decide she will bring him on her evangelism tour. When he return, he has the tongue
of fire.

JENNY: Oh, c'mon—those kind of things only happened in China.

AMA: No—they can happen here as well.

POPO: Di-gou at eight, he goes with See-goh-poh
on her first evangelism tour—they travel all
around Fukien—thirty day and night, preach
to all villages. Five hundred people accept Christ
on these thirty day, and See-goh-poh heal many
sick, restore ear to deaf, put tongue in mouth
of dumb, all these thing and cast out the demon.
Perhaps even one dead man—dead and
wither—he rise up from his sleep. Di-gou see
all this while carry See-goh-poh's bag and bring
her food, ah? After thirty day, they return home.
We have large banquet—perhaps twelve different   dish   that   night—outside—under-
neath—ah—cloth. After we eat, See-goh-poh
say, "Now is time for Family Devotions, and
this time, he will lead." See-goh-poh point to
Di-gou, who is still a boy, but he walk up in
front of table and begin to talk and flame begin

to come from his mouth, over his head. Fire.
Fire, all around. His voice—so loud—praise
and testify the miracle of God. Louder and
louder, more and more fire, till entire sky fill
with light, does not seem to be night, like middle of day, like twelve noon. When he finish
talk, sun has already rise, and cloth over our
head, it is all burn, gone, ashes blow away.
[JOANNE *enters, pulling* CHESTER *behind. He
carries a suitcase.*]

JOANNE: Look who's here!

POPO: Chester—good you decide to come.

JOANNE: He looked lost. This house isn't that big,
you know. [*Exits.*]

AMA: [*To* CHESTER] You come for reunion with Di-
gou. Very good.

CHESTER: Uh—look, I really can't stay. I have to
finish packing.

AMA: You must stay—see Di-gou!

CHESTER: But I'm leaving tomorrow.
[*Doorbell.*]

CHESTER: Oh, no.

JOANNE: Can someone get that? ⎱ [*Simul-*
JENNY: Too late!   ⎰ *taneously*]
POPO: Di-gou!

AMA: [*To* CHESTER] You must! This will be Di-gou!
[WILBUR *crosses with basket, now full of chicken
bones.*]

WILBUR: I'll get it. Chester, good to see you made
it. [*Exits*]

JENNY: He almost didn't.

CHESTER: I'm really short on time. I gotta go. I'll
see you tomorrow at the airport.

POPO: Chester! When Di-gou arrive, he must see
whole family! You stay!

[CHESTER *pauses, decides to stay.*]

CHESTER: [*To* JENNY] This is ridiculous. I can't stay.

JENNY: I always have to. Just grin a lot when you meet this guy. Then everyone will be happy.

CHESTER: I don't wanna meet this guy!

[WILBUR *enters with* HANNAH *and* ROBERT, *who are* CHESTER's *parents.* HANNAH *is* POPO's *daughter. They are five to ten years older than* JOANNE *and* WILBUR.]

WILBUR: [*To* ROBERT] What? What do you mean?

AMA: [*Stands up on a chair; a speech*] Di-gou, thirty year have pass since we last see you—

WILBUR: [*To* AMA] Not now, Ma.

AMA: Do you still love God?

ROBERT: What do you mean, "What do you mean?" That's what I mean.

HANNAH: He wasn't there, Wilbur. [*To* AMA] Auntie! Di-gou isn't with us.

AMA: What? How can this be?

ROBERT: Those Chinese airliners—all junk stuffs—so inefficient.

AMA: Where is he?

POPO: [*To* ROBERT] You sure you look close?

ROBERT: What "look close"? We just waited for everyone to get off the plane.

AMA: Where is he?

HANNAH: [*To* AMA] We don't know, Auntie! [*To* CHESTER] Chester, are you packed?

AMA: Don't know?

CHESTER: [*To* HANNAH] No, I'm not. And I'm really in a hurry.

HANNAH: You're leaving tomorrow! Why aren't you packed?

CHESTER: I'm trying to, Mom.

[ROBERT *pulls out a newspaper clipping, shows it to* CHESTER.]

ROBERT: Look, son, I called the Chinese paper, used a little of my influence—they did a story on you—here.

CHESTER: [*Looks at clipping*] I can't read this, Dad! It's in Chinese!

ROBERT: [*Takes back clipping*] Little joke, there.

AMA: [*To anyone who will listen*] Where is he?

HANNAH: [*To* AMA] Auntie, ask Wilbur. [*To* CHESTER] Get packed!

CHESTER: All right!

WILBUR: [*Trying to explain to* AMA] Well, Mom, they said he wasn't at—

AMA: [*Ignoring* WILBUR *totally*] Where is he?!

[ROBERT *continues to study the newspaper clipping, points a section out to* CHESTER.]

ROBERT: Here—this is where it talks about my bank.

CHESTER: I'm going to pack.

HANNAH: [*To* CHESTER] Going?

CHESTER: [*To* HANNAH] You said I should—

HANNAH: [*To* CHESTER] You have to stay and see Di-gou!

[WILBUR *makes another attempt to explain the situation to* AMA.]

WILBUR: [*To* AMA] See, Mom, I guess—

AMA: [*Ignoring him again*] Where is he?

[ROBERT *continues studying his clipping, oblivious.*]

ROBERT: [*Translating, to* CHESTER] It says, "Great Chinese violinist will conduct and solo with New York Philharmonic."

CHESTER: What? It says what?

HANNAH: [*To* CHESTER] You came without being packed?

[AMA *decides to look for* DI-GOU *on her own, and starts searching the house.*]

AMA: Di-gou! Di-gou!

WILBUR: [*Following* AMA] Ma, listen. I'll explain.

HANNAH: [*To* CHESTER] How can you be so inefficient?

CHESTER: [*To* ROBERT] Dad, I just got a job playing in the violin section in Boston.

AMA: Di-gou! Di-gou!

CHESTER: [*To* ROBERT] I'm not conducting, and—

ROBERT: [*To* CHESTER] Ssssh! I know. But good publicity—for the bank.

HANNAH: [*To* CHESTER] Well, I'll help you pack later. But you have to stay till Di-gou arrives. Sheesh!

CHESTER: I can't believe this!

AMA: [*Continuing her search*] Di-gou! Are you already in bathroom? [*Exits.*]

HANNAH: [*To* AMA] Auntie, he wasn't at the airport! [*To* WILBUR] Why didn't you tell her?

WILBUR: [*Following* AMA] I'm trying! I'm trying! [*Exits.*]

ROBERT: It's those Communist airlines, I'm telling you. Inefficient.

HANNAH: We asked at the desk. They didn't have a flight list.

AMA: [*Entering*] Then where is he?

WILBUR: [*Entering, in despair*] Joanne, will you come here?

ROBERT: They probably left him in Guam.

POPO: [*To* ROBERT] We give you that photograph. You remember to bring it?

ROBERT: Of course I remembered.

HANNAH: [*To* POPO] Mom, it's not Robert's fault.

POPO: [*To* HANNAH] Should leave him [*Refers to* ROBERT] in car.

HANNAH: I tried.

ROBERT: In the car?

HANNAH: He wanted to come in.

ROBERT: It's hot in the car!

AMA: [*To* ROBERT] Suffer, good for you.

POPO: [*To* HANNAH] You cannot control your husband.

ROBERT: I suffer enough.

HANNAH: He said he could help.

POPO: He is wrong again.

AMA: What to do now?

[JENNY *exits in the confusion;* JOANNE *enters.*]

JOANNE: What's wrong now?

WILBUR: They lost your uncle.

JOANNE: Who lost him?

HANNAH: We didn't lose him.

AMA: [*To* ROBERT] You ask at airport desk?

ROBERT: I'm telling you, he's in Guam.

JOANNE: [*To* HANNAH] How could you lose a whole uncle?

HANNAH: We never had him to begin with!

JOANNE: So where is he?

ROBERT: Guam, I'm telling—!

POPO: [*To* ROBERT] Guam, Guam! Shut mouth or go there yourself!

HANNAH: [*A general announcement*] We don't know where he is!

JOANNE: Should I call the police?

WILBUR: You might have looked longer at the airport.

HANNAH: That's what I said, but he [*Refers to* ROBERT] said, "Aaah, too much trouble!"

POPO: [*To* ROBERT] See? You do not care about people from other province besides Shanghai.

ROBERT: [*To* POPO] Mom, I care. It's just that—

POPO: [*To* ROBERT] Your father trade with Japanese during war.

WILBUR: Huh?

ROBERT: Mom, let's not start that—

POPO: Not like our family. We die first!

WILBUR: What's all this about?

ROBERT: Hey, let's not bring up all this other junk, right?

POPO: [*To* ROBERT] You are ashamed.

ROBERT: The airport is a big place.

WILBUR: [*To* ROBERT] Still, you should've been able to spot an old Chinese man.

ROBERT: Everyone on that plane was an old Chinese man!

AMA: True. All Communist look alike.

HANNAH: Hold it, everybody!

[*Pause.*]

Listen, Di-gou has this address, right?

AMA: No.

HANNAH: No? [*To* POPO] Mom, you said he did.

POPO: Yes. He does.

AMA: [*To* POPO] Yes? But I did not write to him.

POPO: I did.

AMA: Now, Communist—they will know this address.

POPO: Never mind.

AMA: No safety. Bomb us.

HANNAH: Okay, he has this address, and he can speak English—after all, he went to medical school here, right? So he shouldn't have any problem.

JOANNE: What an introduction to America.

HANNAH: All we can do is wait.

ROBERT: We went up to all these old Chinese men at the airport, asked them, "Are you our Di-gou?" They all said yes. What could we do? They all looked drunk, bums.

JOANNE: Maybe they're all still wandering through the metal detectors, looking for their families, and will continue till they die.

[CHESTER *wanders onto the tennis court, observes the following section from far upstage.*]

JOANNE: I must have been only about seven the last time Di-gou visited us in the Philippines.

AMA: Less.

JOANNE: Maybe less.

WILBUR: Honey, I'm sure everyone here has a memory, too. You don't see them babbling about it, do you?

JOANNE: The last thing I remember about Di-gou, he was trying to convince you grown-ups to leave the Philippines and return to China. There was a terrible fight—one of the worst that ever took place in our complex. I guess he wanted you to join the Revolution. The fight was so loud that all our servants gathered around the windows to watch.

AMA: They did this?

POPO: Shoot them.

JOANNE: I guess this was just around 1949. Finally, Di-gou left, calling you all sorts of terrible names. On his way out, he set fire to one of our warehouses. All us kids sat around while the servants tried to put it out.

POPO: No. That was not a warehouse.

HANNAH: Yeah, Joanne—the warehouses were concrete, remember?

JOANNE: [*To* HANNAH] But don't you remember a fire?

HANNAH: Yes.

POPO: I think he burn a pile of trash.

ROBERT: [*To* WILBUR] I know how you feel. They're always yap-yap-yapping about their family stories—you'd think they were the only family in China. [*To* HANNAH] I have memories, too.

HANNAH: You don't remember anything. You have a terrible memory.

ROBERT: Look, when I was kidnapped, I didn't know—

HANNAH: Sssssh!

JOANNE: Quiet, Robert!

POPO: Like broken record—ghang, ghang, ghang.

WILBUR: [*To* ROBERT] I tell you what: you wanna take a look at my collection of tax shelters?

ROBERT: Same old stuff?

WILBUR: No. Some new ones.

[*They exit.* DI-GOU *appears on the tennis court; only* CHESTER *sees him, but* CHESTER *says nothing.* CHESTER *watches* DI-GOU *watching the women.*]

JOANNE: Anyway, he set fire to something and the flames burned long into the night. One servant was even killed in it, if I remember correctly. I think Matthew's nursemaid was trying to put it out when her dress caught fire and, like a fool, she ran screaming all over the complex. All the adults were too busy to hear her, I guess, and all the kids just sat there and watched this second fire, moving in circles and screaming.

By morning, both fires were out, and our tutors
came as usual. But that day, nothing func-
tioned just right—I think the water pipes broke
in Sah-Zip's room, the cars wouldn't start—
something—all I remember is servants running around all day with one tool or another.
And that was how Di-gou left Manila for the
last time. Left Manila and returned to China—
in two fires—one which moved—and a great
rush of handymen.

[DI-GOU *is now sitting in their midst in the sunroom. He puts down his suitcase. They turn and
see him. He sticks his thumb out, as if for hitch-
hiking, but it is pointed in the wrong direction.*]

DI-GOU: "Going my way?"

AMA: Di-gou!

DI-GOU: "Hey, baby, got a lift?"

POPO: You see? Our family members will always
return.

JOANNE: [*To* DI-GOU] Are you—? Oh, you're—?
Well, nice—How did you get here?

DI-GOU: [*Pulls a book out of his jacket*] Our diplomacy handbook. Very useful.

POPO: Welcome to America!

DI-GOU: [*Referring to the handbook*] It says, "When
transportation is needed, put your thumb as if
to plug a hole."

AMA: [*On chair*] Di-gou, thirty year have passed—

DI-GOU: [*Still reading*] "And say, 'Going my way?'"

AMA: Do you still believe in God?

DI-GOU: "Or, 'Hey, baby, got a lift?'"

AMA: Do you?

HANNAH: [*To* AMA] Auntie, he's explaining something.

DI-GOU: It worked! I am here!

AMA: [*Getting down off chair*] Still as stubborn as before.

DI-GOU: Hello, my sisters.

POPO: Hello, Di-gou. This is my daughter, Hannah.

HANNAH: [*To* DI-GOU] Were you at the airport? We were waiting for you.

DI-GOU: Hannah. Oh, last time, you were just a baby.

AMA: [*Introducing* JOANNE] And Joanne, remember?

JOANNE: Hello, Di-gou. How was your flight?

DI-GOU: Wonderful, wonderful.

POPO: Where is Chester? Chester! [CHESTER *enters the lanai*.] Him—this is number one grandson.

DI-GOU: Oh, you are Chester. You are the violinist, yes?

CHESTER: You're Di-gou?

DI-GOU: Your parents are so proud of you.

HANNAH: We are not. He's just a kid who needs to pack.

AMA: Where is Jenny? Jenny!

HANNAH: [*To* DI-GOU] We figured you'd be able to get here by yourself.

DI-GOU: Oh, yes. [*He sticks out his thumb.* JENNY *enters.*]

JOANNE: Jenny! Say, "Hi, Di-gou."

JENNY: Hi, Di-gou.

DI-GOU: [*To* JOANNE] This is your daughter?

JOANNE: Yes. Jenny. [*Pause*] Jenny, say, "Hi, Di-gou."

JENNY: Mom, I just did!

JOANNE: Oh. Right.

JENNY: Will you cool out?

DI-GOU: Jenny, the last time I saw your mother, she was younger than you are now.

JENNY: He's kinda cute.

JOANNE: Jenny, your granduncle is not cute.

DI-GOU: Thank you.

JENNY: [*To* JOANNE] Can I go now?

AMA: Why you always want to go?

JENNY: Sorry, Ama. Busy.

JOANNE: [*Allowing* JENNY *to leave*] All right.

DI-GOU: [*To* JENNY] What are you doing?

JENNY: Huh? Reading.

DI-GOU: Oh. Schoolwork.

JENNY: Nah. *Vogue.* [*Exits.*]

JOANNE: I've got to see about dinner. [*To* HANNAH] Can you give me a hand? I want to use my new Cuisinart.

HANNAH: All right. What do you want to make?

JOANNE: I don't know. What does a Cuisinart do? [HANNAH *and* JOANNE *exit;* DI-GOU, AMA, POPO, *and* CHESTER *are left in the sunroom.*]

AMA: Di-gou, thirty year have pass. Do you still love God?

DI-GOU: Thirty-three.

AMA: Ah?

POPO: 1949 to 1982. Thirty-three. He is correct.

AMA: Oh. But you do still love God? Like before?

DI-GOU: You know, sisters, after you left China, I learned that I never did believe in God. [*Pause.*]

AMA: What!

POPO: How can you say this?

CHESTER: Amā, Popo, don't start in on that—he just got here.

POPO: You defend him?

AMA: [*Chasing* CHESTER *out to tennis court*] You both are influence by bad people.

POPO: Spend time with bums! Communist bum, musician bum, both same.

DI-GOU: Just to hear my sisters after all these years—you may speak whatever you like.

AMA: Do you still love God?

DI-GOU: I have much love.

AMA: For God?

DI-GOU: For my sisters.

[*Pause.*]

POPO: You are being very difficult.

AMA: You remember when you first become Christian?

POPO: You travel with See-goh-poh on her first evangelism tour? Before we move to Philippines and you stay in China? Remember? You speak in tongues of fire.

DI-GOU: I was only eight years old. That evening is a blur to me.

AMA: Tonight—we have family devotions. You can speak again. Miracles. You still believe in miracles?

DI-GOU: It is a miracle that I am here again with you!

POPO: Why you always change subject? You remember Ah Hong? Your servant? How See-goh-poh cast out his opium demon?

DI-GOU: I don't think that happened.

AMA: Yes! Remember? After evangelism tour—she cast out his demon.

POPO: Ah Hong tell stories how he eats opium, then he can see everything so clear, like—uh—glass. He can see even through wall, he say, and can see—ah—all the way through floor.

Yes! He say he can see through ground, all the
way to hell. And he talk with Satan and demon
who pretend to be Ah Hong's dead uncles. You
should remember.

DI-GOU: I vaguely recall some such stories.

[DI-GOU *opens up his suitcase during* POPO's *following speech and takes out two small Chinese
toys and a small Chinese flag. He shows them
to* POPO, *but she tries to ignore them.*]

POPO: Demon pretend to be ghost, then show himself everyplace to Ah Hong—in kitchen, in well,
in barn, in street of village. Always just sit
there, never talk, never move, just sit. So See-
goh-poh come, call on God, say only, "Demon
begone."

AMA: And from then on, no more ghost, no more
opium.

POPO: You—you so happy, then. You say, you will
also cast out the demon.

DI-GOU: We were all just children. [*He lines the
toys up on the floor.*]

AMA: But you have faith of a child.

DI-GOU: Ah Hong didn't stop eating opium, though.
He just needed money. That's why two years
later, he was fired.

AMA: Ah Hong never fired!

POPO: I do not think so.

DI-GOU: Yes, my tenth, eleventh birthday, he was
fired.

AMA: No—remember? Ah Hong die many year
later—just before you come to America for college.

DI-GOU: No, he was fired before then.

POPO: No. Before you leave, go to college, you must

prepare your own suitcase. [*To* AMA] Bad memory.

AMA: Brainwash.

[ROBERT *and* WILBUR *enter;* CHESTER *exits off the tennis court.* ROBERT *and* WILBUR *surround* DI-GOU.]

ROBERT *and* WILBUR: Welcome!

WILBUR: How you doing, Di-gow?

ROBERT: [*Correcting* WILBUR] Di-gou!

WILBUR: Oh, right. "Di-gou."

ROBERT: [*To* DI-GOU] We tried to find you at the airport.

WILBUR: [*To* DI-GOU] That means "second brother."

ROBERT: So, you escaped the Communists, huh?

WILBUR: Robert and I were just—

ROBERT: Little joke, there.

WILBUR: —looking at my collection of tax shelters.

ROBERT: China's pretty different now, huh?

WILBUR: You care to take a look?

ROBERT: I guess there's never a dull moment—

WILBUR: Probably no tax shelters, either.

ROBERT: —waiting for the next cultural revolution.

WILBUR: Oh, Robert!

ROBERT: Little joke, there.

WILBUR: [*To* DI-GOU] That's how he [*Refers to* ROBERT] does business.

ROBERT: Of course, I respect China.

WILBUR: He says these totally outrageous things.

ROBERT: But your airlines—so inefficient.

WILBUR: And people remember him.

ROBERT: How long were you in Guam?

WILBUR: [*To* ROBERT] He wasn't in Guam!

ROBERT: No?

WILBUR: [*To* DI-GOU] Well, we're going to finish up the tour.

ROBERT: My shelters are all at my house.

WILBUR: Feel welcome to come along.

ROBERT: His [*Refers to* WILBUR] are kid stuff. Who wants land in Montana?

WILBUR: [*To* ROBERT] Hey—I told you. I need the loss.

[WILBUR *and* ROBERT *exit, leaving* DI-GOU *with* AMA *and* POPO. *There is a long silence.*]

DI-GOU: Who are they?

POPO: Servants.

AMA: Don't worry. They will eat outside. In America, servants do not take over their masters' house.

DI-GOU: What are you talking about?

AMA: We know. In China now, servants beat their masters.

DI-GOU: Don't be ridiculous. I have a servant. A chauffeur.

[ROBERT *reenters.*]

ROBERT: Hey, Di-gou—we didn't even introduce ourselves.

DI-GOU: Oh, my sisters explained it to me.

ROBERT: I'm Robert. Hannah's my wife. [ROBERT *puts his arm around* DI-GOU.] When we married, I had nothing. I was working in grocery stores, fired from one job after another. But she could tell—I had a good heart.

DI-GOU: It is good to see servants marrying into the moneyed ranks. We are not aware of such progress by even the lowest classes.

[*Pause.*]

ROBERT: Huh?

DI-GOU: To come to this—from the absolute bottom of society.

ROBERT: Wait, wait. I mean, sure, I made progress, but "the bottom of society"? That's stretching it some, wouldn't you say?

DI-GOU: Did you meet Hannah while preparing her food?

ROBERT: Huh? No, we met at a foreign students' dance at UCLA.

DI-GOU: Oh. You attended university?

ROBERT: Look, I'm not a country kid. It's not like I was that poor. I'm from Shanghai, you know.

POPO: [*To* ROBERT] Ssssh! Neighbors will hear!

ROBERT: I'm cosmopolitan. So when I went to college, I just played around at first. That's the beauty of the free-enterprise system, Di-gou. If you wanna be a bum, it lets you be a bum. I wasted my time, went out with all those American girls.

POPO: One girl.

ROBERT: Well, one was more serious, a longer commitment...

POPO: Minor.

DI-GOU: What?

POPO: He go out with girl—only fifteen year old.

ROBERT: I didn't know!

POPO: [*To* ROBERT] How come you cannot ask?

ROBERT: I was just an FOB. This American girl— she talked to me—asked me out—kissed me on first date—and I thought, "Land of opportunity!" Anyway, I decided to turn my back on China.

POPO: [*To* DI-GOU] He cannot even ask girl how old.

ROBERT: This is my home. When I wanted to stop being a bum, make money, it let me. That's America!

DI-GOU: I also attended American university. Columbia Medical School.

ROBERT: Right. My wife told me.

POPO: [*To* ROBERT] But he does not date the minor!

ROBERT: [*To* POPO] How was I supposed to know? She looked fully developed!

[AMA *and* POPO *leave in disgust, leaving* ROBERT *alone with* DI-GOU.]

ROBERT: [*To* DI-GOU] Well, then, you must understand American ways.

DI-GOU: It has been some time since I was in America.

ROBERT: Well, it's improved a lot, lemme tell you. Look, I have a friend who's an immigration lawyer. If you want to stay here, he can arrange it.

DI-GOU: Oh, no. The thought never even—

ROBERT: I know, but listen. I did it. Never had any regrets. We might be able to get your family over, too.

DI-GOU: Robert, I cannot leave China.

ROBERT: Huh? Look, Di-gou, people risk their lives to come to America. If only you could talk to—to the boat people.

DI-GOU: Uh—the food here looks very nice.

ROBERT: Huh? Oh, help yourself, Go ahead.

DI-GOU: Thank you. I will wait.

ROBERT: No, go on!

DI-GOU: Thank you, but—

ROBERT: Look, in America, there's so much, we don't have to be polite at all!

DI-GOU: Please—I'm not yet hungry.

ROBERT: Us Chinese, we love to eat, right? Well, here in America, we can be pigs!

DI-GOU: I'm not hungry.

ROBERT: I don't see why you can't—? Look. [*He picks up a piece of food, a* bao.] See? [*He stuffs the whole thing into his mouth.*] Pigs!

DI-GOU: Do you mind? I told you, I'm not—

ROBERT: I know. You're not hungry. Think I'm hungry? No, sir! What do I have to do to convince you? Here. [*He drops a tray of guo-tieh on the ground, begins stomping them.*] This is the land of plenty!

DI-GOU: Ai! Robert!

[ROBERT *continues stomping them like roaches.*]

ROBERT: There's one next to your foot! [*He stomps it.*] Gotcha!

DI-GOU: Please! It is not right to step on food!

ROBERT: "Right?" Now, see, that's your problem in the P.R.C.—lots of justice, but you don't produce.

[WILBUR *enters, catching* ROBERT *in the act.*]

WILBUR: Robert? What are you—? What's all this?

ROBERT: [*Stops stomping*] What's the big deal? You got a cleaning woman, don't you?

[JENNY *enters.*]

JENNY: Time to eat yet? [*She sees the mess.*] Blaagh.

[HANNAH *enters.*]

HANNAH: What's all this?

JENNY: Never mind.

[JENNY *exits;* WILBUR *points to* ROBERT, *indicating to* HANNAH *that* ROBERT *is responsible for the mess.* AMA *and* POPO *also enter at this moment, and see* WILBUR's *indication.*]

DI-GOU: In China, the psychological problems of wealth are a great concern.

POPO: Ai! Who can clean up after man like this!

WILBUR: Robert, I just don't think this is proper.

AMA: Wilbur—not clean himself.

ROBERT: Quiet! You all make a big deal out of nothing!

DI-GOU: I am a doctor. I understand.

POPO: But Robert—he also has the fungus feet.

ROBERT: Shut up, everybody! Will you all just shut up? I was showing Di-gou American ways!

[WILBUR *takes* DI-GOU's *arm.*]

WILBUR: [*To* DI-GOU] Uh—come out here. I'll show you some American ways.

[WILBUR *and* DI-GOU *go out to the tennis court.*]

ROBERT: [*To* WILBUR] What do you know about American ways? You were born here!

POPO: [*To* AMA] Exercise—good for him.

ROBERT: Only us immigrants really know American ways!

POPO: [*To* AMA, *pinching her belly*] Good for here.

HANNAH: [*To* ROBERT] Shut up, dear. You've done enough damage today.

[WILBUR *gets* DI-GOU *a racket.*]

AMA: [*To* POPO] In China, he [*Refers to* DI-GOU] receives plenty exercise. Whenever Communists, they come torture him.

WILBUR: [*On tennis court, to* DI-GOU] I'll set up the machine. [*He goes* OFF.]

ROBERT: [*In sunroom, looking at tennis court*] What's so American about tennis?

HANNAH: [*To* ROBERT] Yes, dear.

ROBERT: You all ruined it!

HANNAH: You ruined the *guo-tieh,* dear.

ROBERT: What's a few *guo-tieh* in defense of America?

DI-GOU: [*To* WILBUR] I have not played tennis since my college days at Columbia.

ROBERT: [*To* HANNAH] He [*refers to* DI-GOU] was being so cheap! Like this was a poor country!

HANNAH: He's lived in America before, dear.

ROBERT: That was years ago. When we couldn't even buy a house in a place like this.

HANNAH: We still can't.

ROBERT: What?

HANNAH: Let's face it. We still can't afford—

ROBERT: That's not what I mean, stupid! I mean, when we wouldn't be able to because we're Chinese! He doesn't know the new America. I was making a point and you all ruined it!

HANNAH: Yes, dear. Now let's go in and watch the Betamax.

ROBERT: No!

HANNAH: C'mon! [ROBERT *and* HANNAH *exit.*] *On the tennis court,* DI-GOU *and* WILBUR *stand next to each other, facing offstage. A machine offstage begins to shoot tennis balls at them, each ball accompanied by a small explosive sound. A ball goes by;* DI-GOU *tries to hit it, but it is too high for him. Two more balls go by, but they are also out of* DI-GOU's *reach. A fourth ball is shot out, which hits* WILBUR.

WILBUR: Aaaah!

[*Balls are being shot out much faster now, pummeling* WILBUR *and* DI-GOU. AMA *and* POPO *continue to sit in the sunroom, staring away from the tennis court, peaceful and oblivious.*]

DI-GOU: Aaah!

WILBUR: I don't—! This never happened—!

DI-GOU: Watch out!

WILBUR: I'll turn off the machine.

DI-GOU: Good luck! Persevere! Overcome! Oh! Watch—!

[*A volley of balls drives* WILBUR *back.* AMA *and* POPO *hear the commotion, look over to the tennis court. The balls stop shooting out.*]

ROBERT: Tennis.

AMA: A fancy machine.

[*They return to looking downstage. The balls begin again.*]

WILBUR: Oh, no!

AMA: Wilbur—he is such a bad loser.

POPO: Good exercise, huh? His age—good for here.

[*She pinches her belly.*]

DI-GOU: I will persevere!

[DI-GOU *tries to get to the machine, is driven back.*]

WILBUR: No! Di-gow!

DI-GOU: I am overcome!

WILBUR: Joanne!

[*He begins crawling like a guerrilla toward the machine and finally makes it offstage. The balls stop, presumably because* WILBUR *reached the machine.* DI-GOU *runs off the court.*]

DI-GOU: [*Breathless*] Is it time yet...that we may cease to have...such enjoyment?

[WILBUR *crosses back onto the tennis court and into the lanai.*]

WILBUR: [*To offstage*] Joanne! This machine's too fast. I don't pay good money to be attacked by my possessions! [*Exits.*]

[AMA *and* POPO *get up, exit into the house, applauding* DI-GOU *as they go, for his exercise.*]

AMA *and* POPO: [*Clapping*] Good, good, very good!

[DI-GOU *is left alone on the tennis court. He is*

hit by a lone tennis ball. CHESTER *enters, with a violin case. It is obvious that he has thrown that ball.*]

CHESTER: Quite a workout, there.

DI-GOU: America is full of surprises—why do all these products function so poorly?

CHESTER: Looks like "Made in U.S." is gonna become synonymous with defective workmanship. [*Pause*] You wanna see my violin?

DI-GOU: I would love to.

CHESTER: I thought you might. Here. [*He removes the violin from its case.*]

CHESTER: See? No "Made in U.S." label.

DI-GOU: It is beautiful.

CHESTER: Careful! The back has a lacquer which never dries—so don't touch it, or you'll leave your fingerprints in it forever.

DI-GOU: Imagine that. After I die, someone could be playing a violin with my fingerprint.

CHESTER: Funny, isn't it?

DI-GOU: You know, I used to play violin.

CHESTER: Really?

DI-GOU: Though I never had as fine an instrument as this.

CHESTER: Try it. Go ahead.

DI-GOU: No. Please. I get more pleasure looking at it than I would playing it. But I would get the most pleasure hearing you play.

CHESTER: No.

DI-GOU: Please?

CHESTER: All right. Later. How long did you play?

DI-GOU: Some years. During the Cultural Revolution, I put it down.

CHESTER: Must've been tough, huh? [CHESTER *directs* DI-GOU*'s attention to the back of his violin.*]

Look—the back's my favorite part.

DI-GOU: China is my home, my work. I had to stay there. [DI-GOU *looks at the back of the violin.*] Oh—the way the light reflects—look. And I can see myself in it.

CHESTER: Yeah. Nice, huh?

DI-GOU: So you will take this violin and make music around the world.

CHESTER: Around the world? Oh, you probably got a misleading press clipping. See, my dad...

DI-GOU: Very funny.

CHESTER: [*Smiling*] Yeah. See, I'm just playing in the Boston Symphony. I'm leaving tomorrow.

DI-GOU: I am fortunate, then, to come today, or perhaps I would never meet you.

CHESTER: You know, I wasn't even planning to come here.

DI-GOU: That would be terrible. You know, in China, my wife and I had no children—for the good of the state.

[DI-GOU *moves to where he left the Chinese toys earlier in the act. He picks them up and studies them.*]

DI-GOU: All these years, I try to imagine—what does Hannah look like? What does her baby look like? Now, I finally visit and what do I find? A young man. A violinist. The baby has long since disappeared. And I learn I'll never know the answer to my question.

[*Silence.*]

CHESTER: Di-gou, why did you come here?

DI-GOU: My wife has died, I'm old. I've come for my sisters.

CHESTER: Well, I hope you're not disappointed to

come here and see your sisters, your family, carry on like this.

DI-GOU: They are still my sisters.

CHESTER: I'm leaving here. Like you did.

DI-GOU: But, Chester, I've found that I cannot leave the family. Today—look!—I follow them across an ocean.

CHESTER: You know, they're gonna start bringing you to church.

DI-GOU: No. My sisters and their religion are two different things.

CHESTER: No, they're not. You've been away. You've forgotten. This family breathes for God. Ever since your aunt, See-goh-poh.

DI-GOU: See-goh-poh is not the first member of this family.

CHESTER: She's the first Christian.

DI-GOU: There are faces back further than you can see. Faces long before the white missionaries arrived in China. Here. [*He holds* CHESTER's *violin so that its back is facing* CHESTER, *and uses it like a mirror.*] Look here. At your face. Study your face and you will see—the shape of your face is the shape of faces back many generations—across an ocean, in another soil. You must become one with your family before you can hope to live away from it.

CHESTER: Oh, sure, there're faces. But they don't matter here. See-goh-poh's face is the only one that has any meaning here.

DI-GOU: No. The stories written on your face are the ones you must believe.

CHESTER: Stories? I see stories, Di-gou. All around me. This house tells a story. The days of the week tell a story.—Sunday is service, Wednesday and Friday are fellowship, Thursday is visitation. Even the furniture tells stories. Look around. See-goh-poh is sitting in every chair. There's nothing for me here.

DI-GOU: I am here.

CHESTER: You? All right. Here. [CHESTER *turns the back of the violin toward* DI-GOU, *again using it like a mirror.*] You look. You wanna know what I see? I see the shape of your face changing. And with it, a mind, a will, as different as the face. If you stay with them, your old self will go, and in its place will come a new man, an old man, a man who'll pray.

DI-GOU: Chester, you are in America. If you deny those whose share your blood, what do you have in this country?

AMA: [*From offstage*] All right? Ready?

CHESTER: Your face is changing, Di-gou. Before you know it, you'll be praying and speaking in tongues.

AMA: [*Still offstage*] One, two, three, four!
   [*The "Hallelujah Chorus" begins. The choir enters, consisting of* WILBUR, JOANNE, ROBERT, HANNAH, *and* POPO. *They are led by* AMA, *who stands at a movable podium which is being pushed into the room by* ROBERT *and* WILBUR *as they sing. (The choir heads for the center of the room, where the podium comes to rest, with* AMA *still on it, and the "Hallelujah Chorus" ends.)* ROBERT *begins singing the tenor aria "Every Valley Shall Be Exalted," from Handel's* Messiah.]

ROBERT: "Every valley, every valley..."

HANNAH: Quiet, Robert!

ROBERT: But I want my solo!

JOANNE: [*To* ROBERT] Ssssh! We already decided this.

ROBERT: [*Continuing to sing*] "...shall be exalted..."

JOANNE: [*Yelling offstage*] Jenny!

AMA: [*To* ROBERT] Time for Family Devotions! Set up room!

[*They begin to arrange the room like a congregation hall, with the pulpit up front.*]

ROBERT: But it's a chance to hear my beautiful voice.

JENNY: [*From offstage*] Yeah! What?

POPO: [*To* ROBERT] Hear at home, hear in car. Now set up room.

JOANNE: [*Yelling offstage*] Jenny! Devotions!

JENNY: [*From offstage*] Aw, Mom.

JOANNE: [*Yelling offstage*] Devotions!

JENNY: [*Entering*] All right.

ROBERT: [*To* HANNAH] You know what this is? This is the breakdown of family authority.

HANNAH: [*To* ROBERT] You have all the authority, dear. Now shut up.

[JENNY *goes over to* CHESTER.]

JENNY: Hey, you still here? I thought for sure you'd have split by now.

CHESTER: I will.

JENNY: You gotta take it easier. Do like me. I act all lotus blossom for them. I say, "Hi, uncle this and auntie that." It's easy.

ROBERT: Look—all this free time. [*Sings*] "Every valley..."

POPO: Shoot him!

[*The room is set up.*]

AMA: We begin! Family Devotions!

[AMA *flips a switch. A neon cross is lit up.*]

JENNY: [*To* CHESTER] Looks like a disco.

[*Everyone is seated except* DI-GOU. *The rest of the family waits for him. He walks over and sits down.* AMA *bows down to pray. Everyone bows except* CHESTER *and* DI-GOU, *but since all other eyes are closed, no one notices their noncompliance.* AMA *begins to pray.*]

AMA: Dear Father, when we think of your great mercy to this family, we can only feel so grateful, privilege to be family chose for your work. You claim us to be yours, put your mark on our heart.

[CHESTER *gets up, picks up his violin, gets* DI-GOU's *attention.*]

AMA: Your blessing begin many year ago in China.

[CHESTER *begins playing; his music serves as underscoring to* AMA's *prayer.*]

AMA: When See-goh-poh, she hear your word— from missionary. Your spirit, it touch her heart, she accept you, she speak in tongue of fire.

[CHESTER *begins to move out of the room as he plays.*]

AMA: You continue, bless See-goh-poh. She become agent of God, bring light to whole family, until we are convert, we become shining light for you all through Amoy.

[CHESTER *stops playing, looks at* DI-GOU, *waves good-bye, and exits.* [DI-GOU *gets up, walks to where* CHESTER *was standing before he left, and waves good-bye.*]

AMA: Let us praise your victory over Satan. Praise your power over demon. Praise miracle over our own sinful will. Praise your victory over even our very hearts. Amen.

[AMA *conducts the choir in the ending of the "Hallelujah Chorus." As they sing, she notices* DI-GOU's *chair is empty. She turns and sees him waving. They look at each other as the "Hallelujah Chorus" continues.* CURTAIN.]

END OF ACT ONE

ACT II

*A moment later. As the curtain rises, all are in the
same positions they occupied at the end of Act I.*
AMA *and* DI-GOU *are looking at each other. The
choir ends the "Hallelujah Chorus."* DI-GOU *walks
back toward his chair, and sits.* AMA *notices that*
CHESTER's *seat is empty.*

AMA: Where is Chester?

HANNAH: I heard his violin.

AMA: This is family devotions.

ROBERT: The kid's got a mind of his own.

HANNAH: He probably went home to pack, Auntie.
He's really in a hurry.

JENNY: Can I go look?

AMA: Why everyone want to go?

JENNY: But he forgot his suitcase. [*She points to
the green suitcase, which* CHESTER *has left behind.*]

POPO: [*To* JENNY] Di-gou, he will want to hear you
give testimony.

[JENNY *sits back down.*]

AMA: Now—Special Testimony. Let us tell of God's
blessing! Who will have privilege? Special Testimony! Who will be first to praise?

146

[*Silence.*]

AMA: He is in our presence! Open His arms to us!
[*Silence.*]

AMA: He is not going to wait forever—you know
this! He is very busy!

[ROBERT *stands up, starts to head for podium.*
POPO *notices that* ROBERT *has risen, points to
him.*]

POPO: No! Not him!

AMA: [*To* ROBERT] He is very bored with certain
people who say same thing over and over again.

WILBUR: Why don't we sit down, Robert?

JENNY: C'mon, Uncle Robert.

HANNAH: Dear, forget it, all right?

ROBERT: But she needed someone to start. I just—

POPO: [*To* ROBERT] She did not include you.

WILBUR: Can't you see how bored they are with
that, Robert?

ROBERT: Bored.

WILBUR: Everybody else has forgotten it.

ROBERT: Forgotten it? They can't.

JOANNE: We could if you'd stop talking about it.

ROBERT: But there's something new!

WILBUR: Of course. There always is.

ROBERT: There is!

JOANNE: [*To* WILBUR] Don't pay attention, dear. It
just encourages him.

WILBUR: [*To* JOANNE] Honey, are you trying to advise *me* on how to be diplomatic?

JOANNE: I'm only saying, if you let Hannah—

WILBUR: You're a real stitch, you know that? You
really are.

JOANNE: Hannah's good at keeping him quiet.

ROBERT: Quiet?

WILBUR: [*To* JOANNE] Look, who was voted "Mr.

Congeniality" at the club last week—you or me?

ROBERT: Hannah, who are you telling to be quiet?

HANNAH: Quiet, Robert.

WILBUR: [*To* JOANNE] Afraid to answer? Huh? Who? Who was "Mr. Congeniality"? Tell me— were you "Mr. Congeniality"?

JENNY: [*To* WILBUR] I don't think she stood a chance, Dad.

WILBUR: [*To* JENNY] Who asked you, huh?

JENNY: "Mr. Congeniality," I think.

WILBUR: Don't be disrespectful.

AMA: We must begin Special Testimony! Who is first?

POPO: I talk.

JOANNE: Good.

POPO: Talk from here. [*She stands.*] Long time since we all come here like this. I remember long ago, family leave China—the boat storm, storm, storm, storm, all around, Hannah cry. I think, "Aaah, why we have to leave China, go to Philippines?" But I remember Jonah, when he did not obey God, only then seas become—ah— dangerous. And even after, after Jonah eaten by whale, God provide for him. So if God has plan for us, we live; if not [*She looks at* DI-GOU.] we die. [*She sits.*] Okay. That's all.

[*Everyone applauds.*]

AMA: Very good! Who is next?

ROBERT: I said, I'd be happy to—

HANNAH: How about Jenny?

JENNY: Me?

JOANNE: Sure, dear, c'mon.

JENNY: Oh . . . well . . .

POPO: [*To* DI-GOU] You see—she is so young, but her faith is old.

JENNY: After I do this, can I go see what's happened to Chester?

POPO: [*To* JENNY] First, serve God.

ROBERT: Let her go.

POPO: Then, you may see about Chester.

JENNY: All right. [*She walks to the podium.*]

POPO: [To DI-GOU] I will tell you what each sentence meaning.

DI-GOU: I can understand quite well.

POPO: No. You are not Christian. You need someone—like announcer at baseball game—except announce for God.

JENNY: [*At podium, she begins testimony.*] First, I want to say that I love you all very much. I really do.

POPO: [*To* DI-GOU] That meaning is, she love God.

JENNY: And I appreciate what you've done for me.

POPO: [*To* DI-GOU] She love us because we show her God.

JENNY: But I guess there are certain times when even love isn't enough.

POPO: [*To* DI-GOU] She does not have enough love for you. You are not Christian.

JENNY: Sometimes, even love has its dark side.

POPO: [*To* DI-GOU] That is you.

JENNY: And when you find that side, sometimes you have to leave in order to come back in a better way.

POPO: [*To* DI-GOU] She cannot stand to be around you.

JENNY: Please. Remember what I said, and think about it later.

POPO: [*To* DI-GOU] You hear? Think!

JENNY: Thank you.

[*Everyone applauds.*]

AMA: Good, good.

JENNY: Can I go now?

ROBERT: [*To* HANNAH] What was she talking about?

AMA: [*To* JENNY] Soon, you can be best testifier—
do testimony on TV.

JENNY: Can I go now?

JOANNE: All right, Jenny.

JENNY: Thanks. [*Exits.*]

ROBERT: [*To* POPO] Why don't you interpret for *me?*
I didn't understand what she was talking about.
Not a bit.

POPO: Good.

ROBERT: Good? Don't you want me to be a better
Christian?

POPO: No. Not too good. Do not want to live in
same part of Heaven as you.

ROBERT: Why not? It'll be great, Popo. We can tell
stories, sing—

POPO: In Heaven, hope you live in basement.

ROBERT: Basement? C'mon, Popo, I'm a celebrity.
They wouldn't give me the basement. They'll
probably recognize my diplomacy ability, make
me ambassador.

JOANNE: To Hell?

ROBERT: Well, if that's the place they send am-
bassadors.

POPO: Good. You be ambassador.

AMA: Special Testimony! Who is next?

ROBERT: [*Asking to be recognized*] Ama?

AMA: [*Ignoring him*] Who is next?

ROBERT: Not me. I think Wilbur should speak.

AMA: [*Disgusted*] Wilbur?

WILBUR: Me?

ROBERT: Yeah.

WILBUR: Well, I don't really...

ROBERT: Tell them, Wilbur. Tell them what kind of big stuffs happen to you. Tell them how important you are.

WILBUR: Well, I...

AMA: Would you...like to speak...Wilbur?

WILBUR: Well, I'd be honored, but if anyone else would rather...

ROBERT: We want to hear what you have to be proud of.

WILBUR: All right. [WILBUR *takes the podium;* AMA *scurries away.*] Uh—well, it's certainly nice to see this family reunion. Uh—last week, I was voted Mr. Congeniality at the club.

ROBERT: What papers was it in?

WILBUR: Huh?

ROBERT: Was it in the L.A. *Times?* Front page? Otis Chandler's paper?

HANNAH: [*A rebuff*] Robert!

POPO: [*To* ROBERT] Devotions is not question-and-answer for anyone except God.

ROBERT: God sometimes speaks through people, doesn't He?

POPO: He has good taste. Would not speak through you.

ROBERT: [*Undaunted, to* WILBUR] Show me one newspaper clipping. Just one!

WILBUR: Well, besides the *Valley Green Sheet*...

ROBERT: The *Valley Green Sheet?* Who pays for that? Junk. People line their birdcages with it.

WILBUR: Well, I suppose from a media standpoint, it's not that big a deal.

AMA: [*To* JOANNE] What means "congeniality"?

JOANNE: It means, "friendly," sort of.

ROBERT: [*To* WILBUR] So why are you talking about it? Waste our time?

WILBUR: Look, Robert, it's obviously a token of their esteem.

ROBERT: Junk stuffs. Little thing. Who cares?

AMA: [*To herself*] "Mr. Friendly"?

ROBERT: It's embarrassing. What if clients say to me, "You're a bank president but your relative can only get into the *Valley Green Sheet*?" Makes me lose face. They think my relatives are bums.

AMA: [*To* JOANNE] He is "Mr. Friendly"?

WILBUR: Look, Robert, the business is doing real well. It's not like that's my greatest accomplishment.

AMA: [*To* JOANNE] How can he be "Mr. Friendly"? He always kill and laugh.

JOANNE: Mom!

ROBERT: [*To* WILBUR] Does your business get in the paper?

WILBUR: Computer software happens to be one of the nation's fastest-growing—

ROBERT: So what? Lucky guess. Big deal.

WILBUR: It was an educated choice, not luck!

[ROBERT *gets up, starts to head for the podium.*]

ROBERT: Anyone can make money in America. What's hard is to become...a celebrity.

WILBUR: You're not a celebrity!

ROBERT: Yes, I am. That's the new thing. See, I just wanted to say that—[*He nudges* WILBUR *off the podium, takes his place.*]—when I was kidnapped, I didn't know if I would live or die.

POPO: [*Turns and sees* ROBERT *at the podium*] Huh?

JOANNE: Robert, forget it!

POPO: How did he get up there?

WILBUR: [*To* JOANNE] I'm perfectly capable of handling this myself.

POPO: He sneak up there while we are bored!

WILBUR: [*To* POPO] I'm sorry you found my testimony boring.

ROBERT: [*To* WILBUR] It was. [*To the assemblage*] Now hear mine.

JOANNE: We've all heard it before.

HANNAH: [*To* ROBERT] They're tired, dear. Get down.

ROBERT: Why? They listened to Wilbur's stuff. Boring. Junk.

JOANNE: "I didn't know if I would live or die." "I didn't know if I would live or die."

ROBERT: Di-gou, he hasn't heard. Have you, Di-gou?

DI-GOU: Is this when you didn't know if you would live or die?

ROBERT: How did—? Who told him?

POPO: I cannot think of enough ways to shoot him! Rifle! Arrows!

HANNAH: [*To* ROBERT] Sit down!

ROBERT: But there's something new!

HANNAH: I think we better let him speak, or he'll never shut up.

ROBERT: She's right. I won't.

JOANNE: All right. Make it quick, Robert.

ROBERT: All right. As I was saying, I didn't know if I would live or die.

JOANNE: You lived.

ROBERT: But the resulting publicity has made me a celebrity. Every place I go, people come up to me—"Aren't you the one that got kidnapped?" When I tell them how much the ransom was, they can hardly believe it. They ask for my autograph. Now—here's the new thing. I met these clients last week, told them my story. Now, these guys are big shots and they say it would make a great movie. Yeah. No kidding. They made movies before. Not just regular movie, that's junk stuffs. We want to go where the big money is—we want to make a mini-series for TV. Like "Shogun." I told them, they should take the story, spice it up a little, you know? Add some sex scenes—we were thinking that I could have some hanky-panky with one of my kidnappers—woman, of course—just for audience sake—like Patty Hearst. I told them I should be played by Marlon Brando. And I have the greatest title: "Not a Chinaman's Chance." Isn't that a great title? "Not a China-man's Chance." Beautiful. I can see the beginning already: I'm walking out of my office. I stop to help a man fixing a flat tire.

HANNAH: All right, dear. That's enough.

ROBERT: Meanwhile, my secretary is having sex with my kidnapper.

HANNAH: Kidnap! Kidnap! That's all I ever hear about!

ROBERT: But, Hannah, I didn't know if I would live or die.

HANNAH: I wish you'd never even been kidnapped.

JOANNE: Well, what about Wilbur?

WILBUR: Leave me out of this.

JOANNE: Wilbur, you could be kidnapped.

WILBUR: I know, I know. It just hasn't happened yet, that's all.

HANNAH: Listen, Joanne. Count your blessings. It's not that great a thing. If they live, they never stop talking about it.

ROBERT: But the publicity!—I sign newspapers all the time!

JOANNE: I'm just saying that Robert's not the only one worth kidnapping.

HANNAH: Joanne, no one's saying that.

AMA: Yes. We all desire Wilbur to be kidnapped also.

POPO: And Robert. Again. This time, longer.

JOANNE: I mean, Wilbur has a lot of assets.

ROBERT: Wilbur, maybe next time you can get kidnaped.

WILBUR: Never mind, honey.

JOANNE: You do.

WILBUR: I can defend myself.

ROBERT: But it takes more than assets to be kidnapped. You have to be cosmopolitan.

HANNAH: Hey, wait. What kind of example are we setting for Di-gou?

ROBERT: See? That's why I'm talking about it. To show Di-gou the greatness of America. I'm just an immigrant, Di-gou, an FOB—but in America, I get kidnapped.

HANNAH: I mean, a Christian example.

DI-GOU: Oh, do not worry about me. This is all very fascinating.

JOANNE: [*To* ROBERT] So, you think you're cosmopolitan, huh?

ROBERT: I am. Before they let me loose, those kidnappers—they respected me.

JOANNE: They probably let you go because they couldn't stand to have you in their car.

POPO: Probably you sing to them.

ROBERT: No. They said, "We've been kidnapping a long time, but—"

JOANNE: Because we can't stand to have you in

our house!

[*Pause.*]

ROBERT: [*To* JOANNE] Now what kind of example
are you setting for Di-gou?

WILBUR: Joanne, just shut up, okay?

HANNAH: [*To* DI-GOU] It's not always like this.

JOANNE: [*To* WILBUR] You never let me talk! You
even let him [*Refers to* ROBERT] talk, but you
never let me talk!

AMA: [*To* JOANNE] He [*Refers to* WILBUR] cannot
deprive you of right to speak. Look. No gun.

ROBERT: Joanne, I have to tell this because Di-gou
is here.

DI-GOU: Me?

JOANNE: [*To* ROBERT] You tell it to waiters!

ROBERT: Joanne, I want him [*Refers to* DI-GOU] to
understand America. The American Dream.
From rags to kidnap victim.

JOANNE: [*To* ROBERT] Well, I don't like you making Di-gou think that Wilbur's a bum.

WILBUR: [*To* JOANNE] Dear, he doesn't think that.

JOANNE: [*To* DI-GOU] You see, don't you, Di-gou?
This house. Wilbur bought this.

DI-GOU: It is a palace.

JOANNE: It's larger than Robert's.

HANNAH: Joanne, how can you sink to my husband's level?

ROBERT: My house would be larger, but we had to
pay the ransom.

POPO: Waste of money.

JOANNE: Look, all of you always put down Wilbur.
Well, look at what he's done.

WILBUR: [*To* JOANNE] Just shut up, all right?

JOANNE: [*To* WILBUR] Well, if you're not going to
say it.

WILBUR: I don't need you to be my PR firm.

ROBERT: [*To anybody*] He doesn't have a PR firm. We do. Tops firm.

JOANNE: [*To* WILBUR] Let me say my mind!

WILBUR: There's nothing in your mind worth saying.

JOANNE: What?

WILBUR: Face it, honey, you're boring.

AMA: [*To* WILBUR] At least she does not torture!

WILBUR: Please! No more talking about torture, all right?

AMA: All right. I will be quiet. No need to torture me.

POPO: [*To* DI-GOU] This small family disagreement.

JOANNE: So I'm boring, huh?

WILBUR: [*To* JOANNE] Look, let's not do this here.

POPO: [*To* DI-GOU] But power of God will overcome this.

JOANNE: I'm boring—that's what you're saying?

HANNAH: Joanne! Not in front of Di-gou!

JOANNE: [*To* DI-GOU] All right. You're objective. Who do you think is more boring?

DI-GOU: Well, I can hardly—

WILBUR: Please, Joanne.

POPO: [*To* DI-GOU] Do you understand how power of God will overcome this?

JOANNE: He [*Refers to* WILBUR] spends all his time with machines, and he calls me boring!

AMA: Di-gou, see the trials of this world?

WILBUR: [*To* JOANNE] Honey, I'm sorry, all right?

JOANNE: Sure, you're sorry.

AMA: [*To* DI-GOU] Argument, fight, no-good husbands.

WILBUR: "No-good husbands"?

[ROBERT, *in disgust, exits into the house.*]

AMA: [*To* DI-GOU] Turn your eyes from this.

[POPO *and* AMA *turn* DI-GOU's *eyes from the fight.*]

JOANNE: [*To* WILBUR] She's [*Refers to* AMA] right, you know.

WILBUR: All right, honey, let's discuss this later.

JOANNE: Later! Oh, right.

[WILBUR *runs off into the house;* JOANNE *yells after him.*]

JOANNE: When we're with *your* family, that's when you want to talk about my denting the Ferrari.

HANNAH: Joanne! Don't be so boring!

JOANNE: [*To* HANNAH] With *our* family, it's "later."

AMA: [*To* DI-GOU] Look up to God!

[POPO *and* AMA *force* DI-GOU *to look up.*]

DI-GOU: Please!

[DI-GOU *breaks away from the sisters' grip, but they knock him down.*]

POPO: Now—is time to join family in Heaven.

AMA: Time for you to return to God.

HANNAH: [*To* JOANNE] Look—they're converting Di-gou.

POPO: Return. Join us for eternity.

AMA: Pray now.

[POPO *and* AMA *try to guide* DI-GOU *to the neon cross.*]

DI-GOU: Where are we going?

AMA: He will wash you in blood of the lamb.

POPO: Like when you are a child. Now! You bow down!

HANNAH: Ask God for His forgiveness.

JOANNE: You won't regret it, Di-gou.

DI-GOU: Do you mind? [*He breaks away.*]

POPO: Why will you not accept Him?

AMA: There is no good reason.

DI-GOU: I want to take responsibility for my own life.

POPO: You cannot!

AMA: Satan is rule your life now.

DI-GOU: I am serving the people.

AMA: You are not.

POPO: You serve them, they all die, go to Hell. So what?

DI-GOU: How can you abandon China for this Western religion?

AMA: It is not.

POPO: God is God of all people.

DI-GOU: There is no God!

[*Pause.*]

AMA: There is too much Communist demon in him. We must cast out demon.

POPO: Now, tie him on table.

DI-GOU: This is ridiculous. Stop this.

[*The women grab* DI-GOU, *tie him on the table.*]

POPO: We have too much love to allow demon to live.

DI-GOU: What?

POPO: [*To* JOANNE *and* HANNAH *who are hesitating.*] Now!

DI-GOU: You can't—!

POPO: Now! Or demon will escape!

AMA: We must kill demon.

POPO: Shoot him!

AMA: Kill for good.

POPO: Make demon into *jok!*

DI-GOU: This is barbaric! You live with the barbarians, you become one yourself!

POPO: Di-gou, if we do not punish your body, demon will never leave.

AMA: Then you will return to China.

POPO: And you will die.

AMA: Go to Hell.

POPO: And it will be too late.

DI-GOU: I never expected Chinese children to tie down their elders.

[DI-GOU *is now securely tied to the table.*]

HANNAH: All right. We're ready.

POPO: Now—you give your testimony.

DI-GOU: I'll just lie here and listen, thank you.

AMA: You tell of God's mercies to you.

JOANNE: How He let you out of China.

AMA: Where you are torture.

JOANNE: Whipped.

POPO: After thirty year, He let you out. Praise Him!

DI-GOU: I will never do such a thing!

HANNAH: If you wait too long, He'll lose patience.

POPO: Now—tell of your trip with See-goh-poh.

POPO: The trip which begin your faith.

DI-GOU: I was only eight years old. I don't remember.

POPO: Tell how many were convert on her tour.

HANNAH: Tell them, Di-gou.

DI-GOU: I cannot.

JOANNE: Why? Just tell the truth.

POPO: Tell how you saw the miracle of a great evangelist, great servant of God.

HANNAH: Tell them before they lose their patience.

DI-GOU: I'm sorry. I will not speak.

POPO: Then we are sorry, Di-gou, but we must punish your body. Punish to drive out the demon and make you speak.

HANNAH: Don't make them do this, Di-gou.

AMA: If you will not speak See-goh-poh's stories in language you know, we will punish you until you speak in tongue of fire.

[AMA *hits* DI-GOU *with an electrical cord, using it like a whip.*]

JOANNE: Please, Di-gou!

HANNAH: Tell them!

AMA: Our Lord was beat, nails drive through His body, for our sin. Your body must suffer until you speak the truth.

[AMA *hits him.*]

HANNAH: Tell them, See-goh-poh was a great evangelist.

AMA: You were on her evangelism tour—we were not—you must remember her converts, her miracle.

[*Hit.*]

JOANNE: Just tell them and they'll let you go!

AMA: Think of See-goh-poh! She is sit! [*Hit*] Sit beside God. He is praising her! Praise her for her work in China.

[CHESTER *enters the tennis court; he looks into the sunroom and sees* AMA *hit* DI-GOU.]

AMA: She is watching you!

[*Hit.* CHESTER *tries to get into the sunroom, but the glass door is locked. He bangs on it, but everyone inside stands shocked at* AMA'S *ritual, and no one notices him. He exits off the tennis court, running.*]

AMA: Praying for you! Want you to tell her story! [*Hit.*]

AMA: We will keep you in float. Float for one second between life and death. Float until you lose will to hold to either—hold to anything at all.

[AMA *quickly slips the cord around* DI-GOU'S *neck, begins pulling on it.* JOANNE *and* HANNAH *run to get* AMA *off of* DI-GOU. CHESTER *enters from*

the house, with JENNY *close behind him. He pulls*
AMA *off of* DI-GOU.]

CHESTER: Ama! Stop it!

[DI-GOU *suddenly breaks out of his bonds and
rises up on the table. He grabs* CHESTER. *The
barbecue bursts into flames.* DI-GOU, *holding onto*
CHESTER, *begins speaking in tongues.*]

AMA: [*Looking up from the ground*] He is speaking
in tongues! He has returned!

[*Everyone falls to their knees.*]

[*As* DI-GOU's *tongues continue,* CHESTER *is suddenly filled with words, and begins interpreting*
DI-GOU's *babbling.*]

CHESTER: Di-gou at eight goes with See-goh-poh
on her first evangelism tour. Di-gou and See-
goh-poh traveling through the summer heat to
a small village in Fukien. Sleeping in the straw
next to See-goh-poh. Hearing a sound. A human
sound. A cry in my sleep. Looking up and seeing
a fire. A fire and See-goh-poh. See-goh-poh is
naked. Naked and screaming. Screaming with
legs spread so far apart. So far that a mouth
opens up. A mouth between her legs. A mouth
that is throwing up blood, spitting out blood.
More and more blood. See-goh-poh's hands
making a baby out of the blood. See-goh-poh
hits the blood baby. Hits the baby and the baby
cries. Watching the baby at See-goh-poh's
breast. Hearing the sucking.

[AMA *and* POPO *spring up.*]

POPO: Such a thing never happened!

AMA: See-goh-poh never did this!

POPO: This is not tongues. This is not God. This is
demon!

CHESTER: Sucking. Praying. Sucking. Squeezing. Crying.

AMA: He is possess by demon!

CHESTER: Biting. Blood. Milk.

POPO: Both have the demon!

CHESTER: Blood and milk. Blood and milk running down.

AMA: [*To the other women*] You pray.

CHESTER: Running down, further and further down.

POPO: We must cast out the demon!

[DI-GOU's *tongues slowly become English, first overlapping, then overtaking* CHESTER's *translation.* CHESTER *becomes silent and exhausted, drops to the ground.*]

CHESTER *and* DI-GOU: Down. Down and into the fire. The fire down there. The fire down there.

[DI-GOU *breaks the last of his bonds, gets off the table.*]

DI-GOU: [*To the sisters*] Your stories are dead now that you know the truth.

AMA: We have faith. We know our true family stories.

DI-GOU: You do not know your past.

AMA: Are you willing to match your stories against ours?

[DI-GOU *indicates his willingness to face* AMA, *and the two begin a ritualistic battle.* POPO *supports* AMA *by speaking in tongues.* AMA *and* DI-GOU *square off in seated positions, facing one another.*]

AMA: We will begin. How many rooms in our house in Amoy?

DI-GOU: Eighteen. How many bedrooms?

AMA: Ten. What year was it built?

DI-GOU: 1893. What year was the nineteenth room added?

AMA: 1923.

DI-GOU: On whose instructions?

AMA: See-goh-poh.

DI-GOU: What year did See-goh-poh die?

AMA: 1945. What disease?

DI-GOU: Malaria. How many teeth was she missing?

AMA: Three.

DI-GOU: What villages were on See-goh-poh's evangelism tour?
   [*Silence.*]

DI-GOU: Do you know?

AMA: She preached to all villages in Fukien.

DI-GOU: Name one.
   [*Silence.*]

DI-GOU: Do you know? Your stories don't know. It never happened.

AMA: It did! What year was she baptized? [*Silence*] What year was she baptized?

DI-GOU: She was never baptized.

AMA: You see? You don't remember.

DI-GOU: Never baptized.

AMA: It was 1921. Your stories do not remember.

DI-GOU: Who was converted on her evangelism tour?

AMA: Perhaps five hundred or more.

DI-GOU: Who? Name one.
   [*Silence.*]

AMA: It is not important.

DI-GOU: You see? It never happened.

AMA: It did.

DI-GOU: You do not remember. You do not know the past. See-goh-poh never preached.

AMA: How can you say this?

DI-GOU: She traveled.

AMA: To preach.

DI-GOU: To travel.

AMA: She visited many—

DI-GOU: I was there! She was thrown out—thrown out on her evangelism tour when she tried to preach.

[*Silence.*]

AMA: It does not matter.

DI-GOU: You forced her to invent the stories.

AMA: We demand nothing!

DI-GOU: You expected! Expected her to convert all Amoy!

AMA: She did!

DI-GOU: Expected many miracles.

AMA: She did! She was a great—

DI-GOU: Expected her not to have a baby.

AMA: She had no husband. She had no baby. This is demon talk. Demon talk and lie.

DI-GOU: She turned away from God.

AMA: We will never believe this!

DI-GOU: On her tours she could both please you and see China.

[POPO's *tongues become weaker; she starts to falter.*]

AMA: See-goh-poh was a great—

DI-GOU: Only on her tours could she see both China and her baby.

AMA: She was a great...a great evangelist... many...

DI-GOU: Where is she buried?

AMA: ...many miracle...

DI-GOU: She is not buried within the walls of the church in Amoy.

AMA: ...many miracle a great evangelist...

[POPO *collapses.*]

DI-GOU: In her last moment, See-goh-poh wanted to be buried in Chinese soil, not Christian soil. You don't know. You were in the Philippines. [*Pause.*]

DI-GOU: I come to bring you back to China. Come, sisters. To the soil you've forsaken with ways born of memories, of stories that never happened. Come, sisters. The stories written on your face are the ones you must believe.

[AMA *rises from her chair.*]

AMA: We will never believe this! [*She collapses back into her chair, closes her eyes.*]

[*Silence.*]

DI-GOU: Sisters?

[*Silence.*]

DI-GOU: Sisters!

[JENNY, CHESTER, JOANNE, HANNAH, *and* DI-GOU *stare at the two inert forms.*]

CHESTER: Jenny! Jenny!

[JENNY *goes to* CHESTER's *side.*]

JOANNE: Hannah? Hannah—come here.

[HANNAH *does not move.*]

HANNAH: I see.

JOANNE: No! Come here!

HANNAH: I know, Joanne. I see.

DI-GOU: Once again. Once again my pleas are useless. But now—this is the last time. I have given all I own.

[POPO *and* AMA *have died.* DI-GOU *picks up his suitcase and the Chinese toys, heads for the door.*]

JOANNE: [*To* DI-GOU] Are you leaving?

DI-GOU: Now that my sisters have gone, I learn. No one leaves America. And I desire only to drive an American car—very fast—down an American freeway.

[DI-GOU *exits.*]

JOANNE: [*Yelling after him*] This is our home, not yours! Why didn't you stay in China! This is not your family!

[JENNY *starts to break away from* CHESTER, *but he hangs onto her.* JOANNE *turns, sees the figures of* AMA *and* POPO.]

JOANNE: Wilbur! Wilbur, come here!

JENNY: [*To* CHESTER] Let go of me! Get away! [*She breaks away from* CHESTER.] I don't understand this, but whatever it is, it's ugly and it's awful and it causes people to die. It causes people to die and I don't want to have anything to do with it.

[JENNY *runs out onto the tennis court and away. On her way, she passes* ROBERT, *who has entered onto the court.* ROBERT *walks into the sunroom. Silence.*]

ROBERT: What's wrong with her? She acts like someone just died. [*Silence. He pulls up a chair next to* CHESTER.] Let's chit-chat, okay?

CHESTER: Sure, Dad.

ROBERT: So, how's Dorrie? [*Silence*] How much they paying you in Boston? [*Silence*] Got any new newspaper clippings?

[*Silence.*]

[CHESTER *gets up, picks up his suitcase, walks onto the tennis court, and shuts the glass doors.*]

[AMA *and* POPO *lie in the center of the room.*
JOANNE *and* HANNAH *stare at them.* ROBERT *sits,
staring off into space.*]

[CHESTER *turns around, looks through the glass
door onto the scene.*]

[*The* LIGHTS BEGIN TO DIM *until there is a single
spotlight on* CHESTER'*s face, standing where* DI-
GOU *stood at the beginning of the play.*]

[*The shape of* CHESTER'*s face begins to change.*]

CURTAIN

THE HOUSE OF
SLEEPING BEAUTIES

From the Short Story
by Yasunari Kawabata

For Natolie

This play is a fantasy. In historical fact, Kawabata's composition of his novelette, *House of the Sleeping Beauties,* and his unexplained suicide occurred many years apart.

Many people helped me develop this play, and I'd like to thank especially Grafton Mouen, Jean Brody, John Harnagel, Marcy Mattox, Natolie Miyawaki, Nancy Takahashi, Mitch Motooka, and Helen Merrill.

CHARACTERS

YASUNARI KAWABATA, 72, a leading Japanese novelist.
WOMAN, Japanese, late seventies.

SYNOPSIS OF SCENES

Scene 1. The sitting room of the House of Sleeping Beauties. Night.
Scene 2. The sitting room, following evening.
Scene 3. The sitting room, several months later, evening.
Scene 4. The sitting room, one week later, evening.

TIME: 1972

PLACE: Tokyo

Scene 1

*A sitting room. Not richly decorated. Desk, pillows,
low table, equipment for tea, cabinet, screen, mirror, furnace. Night.* WOMAN *sits at desk, writing.*
KAWABATA *paces.*

WOMAN: Now, you mustn't do anything distasteful.

KAWABATA: Distasteful?

WOMAN: You mustn't stick your fingers in the girl's
mouth, or anything like that.

KAWABATA: Oh, no. I wouldn't think of it.

WOMAN: Good. All my guests are gentlemen.

KAWABATA: Would you please put that down?

WOMAN: [*Indicating the pen*] This?

KAWABATA: Yes. I'm not here to be interviewed.

WOMAN: Perhaps. *I* am, however, accountable to
my girls—

KAWABATA: Fine.

WOMAN: —and must therefore ask a few questions
of those who wish to become my guests.

KAWABATA: You assume too easily, madame.

WOMAN: Oh?

KAWABATA: You assume that my presence here
identifies me as just one type of man.

WOMAN: On the contrary, sir.

172

KAWABATA: Why did you assume I was going in there, then?

WOMAN: I never assumed any such thing. Did you assume I was going to allow you in there? [*Pause.*]

KAWABATA: "Allow me"?

WOMAN: Actually, I identify two types of men, sir— gentlemen and those who do not behave. My guests are all gentlemen. They do not disgrace the house. Obviously, very few men meet these requirements.

KAWABATA: What are you talking about?

WOMAN: I must protect my girls, and the house.

KAWABATA: Well, I mean, I'm certainly not going to assault a girl, if that's what you mean. Is that what you think? That I look like a man who goes to brothels?

WOMAN: Neither looks nor brothels has much to do with it, sir. My experience has taught me that in most cases, scratch a man and you'll find a molester.

KAWABATA: Well, if you take that kind of attitude...

WOMAN: A look in most men's bottom drawers confirms this.

KAWABATA: ...how is any man to prove he's a...a gentleman, as you say?

WOMAN: I take a risk on all my guests. But I have my methods; I judge as best I can.

KAWABATA: That's ridiculous. That men must be...tested to become your customers. But all your customers are practically ghosts anyway—of course they don't object. Their throats are too dry to protest.

WOMAN: Guests.

KAWABATA: I'm sorry?

WOMAN: They're not customers, they're guests.

KAWABATA: Well, I, for one, do not intend to become a guest, understand?

WOMAN: You are very proud.

KAWABATA: Proud?

WOMAN: But that doesn't necessarily mean you are not a gentleman. Sometimes the proudest men are the best behaved. So, you don't want to be my guest. What *do* you want?

KAWABATA: I only want to talk.

WOMAN: About what?

KAWABATA: Your house.

WOMAN: Shopping?

KAWABATA: No.

WOMAN: I'm sorry.

KAWABATA: I want to know why the old men come here.

WOMAN: But all your answers are in there.

KAWABATA: No, they're not. I could never feel what they feel, what brings them back—a parade of corpses—night after night. But you—perhaps they share their secrets.

WOMAN: I have no secrets.

KAWABATA: Old Eguchi—

WOMAN: And I'm no gossip.

KAWABATA: He talked to me last week.

WOMAN: Yes, he called and said you were coming.

KAWABATA: Said he comes here almost every night. I wanted him to tell me more, but he said I could only know more by talking to you.

WOMAN: He said you wished to gain entrance.

KAWABATA: No—he's making the same mistake as you. I won't be able to feel what he feels because my mind's different.

WOMAN: Oh?

KAWABATA: Eguchi's so old.

WOMAN: And you're young?

KAWABATA: Well, no. Not in years.

WOMAN: Oh.

KAWABATA: But my mind is young. Eguchi's is gone. He sits on his *futon* each afternoon swatting bees with tissue paper. Listen, I know you're a woman of business—may I offer you some fee for what you know?

WOMAN: Money?

KAWABATA: Don't worry. I'm not with the police or anything.

WOMAN: Don't be ridiculous. What do you take me for?

KAWABATA: What do I—?

WOMAN: You might as well pay me to tell you how one falls in love.

KAWABATA: What do you take yourself for, madame—acting like a sorceress, a *sensei*. You're just an old woman running this house. I have questions, and I'm willing to pay for the answers.

WOMAN: I have questions also. Fair, sir? [*Pause*] How old are you?

KAWABATA: I won't answer just anything, you know.

WOMAN: Don't worry. Neither will I.

KAWABATA: Seventy-two.

WOMAN: Married?

KAWABATA: My wife passed away...several years ago.

WOMAN: I'm sorry. Children?

KAWABATA: Yes. Two. Daughters. Why are you asking this?

WOMAN: Don't worry. I'm no gossip. Retired?

KAWABATA: Uh—no...I mean, yes.

WOMAN: Yes or no?

KAWABATA: Uh—no.

WOMAN: No? No. Profession?

KAWABATA: Uh—teacher.

WOMAN: Teacher.

KAWABATA: University level, of course.

WOMAN: There. That wasn't so bad, was it?

KAWABATA: That's all?

WOMAN: Now, what would *you* like to know?

KAWABATA: From that, you decide?

WOMAN: I *would* like you to join me in a game, though.

KAWABATA: A game?

WOMAN: Yes. And as we play, we can talk about the rooms. Do you mind?

KAWABATA: Well, if it's harmless.

WOMAN: Quite. Would you like some tea?

KAWABATA: Oh, yes. Please. Thank you. This game—what's it called?

WOMAN: I don't know. It's old. Geishas used to play it with their customers, to relax them. [*She brings the tea, pours it.*]

KAWABATA: Relax? Perhaps it will relax me. [*He laughs softly.*] Now, why do you want me to play this?

[*She pulls out of the desk a box, and opens it. Inside are twenty-five smooth tiles, five times as long as they are wide. While she speaks, she stacks them in five layers of five tiles each, such that the tiles of each layer are perpendicular to those of the layer below it.*]

WOMAN: So we can get to know each other. As I

said, I must protect my girls from men who do
not behave.

KAWABATA: You talk as if men should be put on
leashes.

WOMAN: No, leashes aren't necessary at all. [*The
tower is finished.*] There. We'll take turns re-
moving tiles from the tower until it collapses.
Understand?

KAWABATA: Is this a game you ask all your customers to play?

WOMAN: Guests. You can't touch the top layer,
though, and you can only use one hand.

KAWABATA: But what's the object? Who wins, who
loses?

WOMAN: There are no winners or losers. There is
only the tower—intact or collapsed. Just one
hand—like this. [*She removes a piece.*]

KAWABATA: My turn? What am I trying to do?

WOMAN: Judge the tiles. Wriggle that one, for instance—yes, that one you're touching—between your fingers. Is the weight of the stack
on it? If so, don't force it. Leave it and look for
another one that's looser. If you try to force the
tiles to be what they're not, the whole thing
will come crashing down.

KAWABATA: A test of skills? There [*He removes a
piece.*]—your turn.

WOMAN: See? Simple.

KAWABATA: What kind of a test—? You're just an
old woman. What kind of a contest is this?

WOMAN: Let's talk about you, sir. We want to make
you happy.
[*They continue to take turns through the following section.*]

KAWABATA: Happy? No, you don't understand. You can't—

WOMAN: Our guests sleep much better here. It's the warmth, they say.

KAWABATA: I don't have any trouble sleeping.

WOMAN: Don't you?

KAWABATA: Sometimes...sometimes I choose not to go to bed. But when I do, I sleep.

WOMAN: Our guests are never afraid to go to sleep.

KAWABATA: It's not that I'm afraid.

WOMAN: The darkness does not threaten them. [*Pause.*]

KAWABATA: Old Eguchi—he says that the girls ...that they are naked.

WOMAN: Yes.

KAWABATA: He says they are very beautiful, but I hardly...

WOMAN: For you, I would pick an especially pretty one.

KAWABATA: For me—? Don't start—

WOMAN: How old was your wife when you first met her?

KAWABATA: My wife? Oh, I don't know. She must have been—oh, maybe nineteen.

WOMAN: Nineteen. That is a beautiful age. I would pick one who is nineteen.

KAWABATA: Don't be ridiculous. She'd see me and—

WOMAN: But you forget, sir—our girls won't see anything.

KAWABATA: I suppose you have some way of guaranteeing this. I suppose it's never happened that some girl has opened her eyes—

WOMAN: No. Never.

[KAWABATA *is having a particularly difficult time with a tile.*]

KAWABATA: Look at this. [*He holds out his hand, laughs.*] Shaking. Would you mind putting some more wood in the furnace?

WOMAN: Of course. [*She does so as she talks.*] I know what girl I would pick for you. She is half Japanese, half Caucasian. She has the most delicate hair—brown in one light, black in another. As she sleeps, she wriggles her left foot, like a cat, against the mattress, as if to draw out even the last bits of warmth.

[*She returns to the table, sits. As she does,* KAWABATA *causes the tower to fall.*]

KAWABATA: Ai! You shook it.

WOMAN: No.

[*During the next section, she gets up, goes to the cabinet, removes a small jar filled with clear liquid and a tiny cup. She pours the liquid into the cup.*]

KAWABATA: Maybe an accident, but still—

WOMAN: I assure you.

KAWABATA: —when you sat down.

WOMAN: I was perfectly still.

KAWABATA: No, you shook the table.

WOMAN: I didn't touch it.

KAWABATA: Just a bit.

WOMAN: Really.

KAWABATA: But at the crucial moment.

WOMAN: Please, sir.

KAWABATA: Just as it was about to give.

WOMAN: Thank you for playing.

KAWABATA: It wasn't fair.

WOMAN: Please—

KAWABATA: It was my first time.

WOMAN: —take this cup.

KAWABATA: What?

WOMAN: Here.

[*He takes it.*]

KAWABATA: What is this?

WOMAN: To help you sleep.

KAWABATA: Sleep?

WOMAN: To assure you a restful evening—in there. [*Pause*] If you wish to, you may now go in. You're my guest. If you still have questions after tonight, I'll try to answer some—

KAWABATA: I can just—

WOMAN: —on your next visit.

KAWABATA: —go in?

WOMAN: Welcome. Your name?

KAWABATA: My name?

WOMAN: We keep names of all our guests.

KAWABATA: But I don't see why...

WOMAN: Our guests are our friends. Sometimes we like to let our friends know if we have something special. Don't worry. Confidential.

KAWABATA: Kawabata.

WOMAN: May I help you undress, Mr. Kawabata?

KAWABATA: Oh, yes. Thank you. [*They go behind the screen.*] I can just...go in?

WOMAN: Yes. On the right, second door. [*Pause*] She's a very pretty girl.

KAWABATA: Second door.

WOMAN: On the right. She's asleep, waiting for you.

[*Pause.*]

KAWABATA: I'm really only curious.

WOMAN: I know. That's why you should go in.

KAWABATA: What if...something happens?

WOMAN: Something?

KAWABATA: What if she wakes up?

WOMAN: Even if you were to try your utmost—you could cut off her arms and she wouldn't wake up till morning. Don't worry. [*They come out from behind the screen. He wears a light robe.*] Sleep well, Mr. Kawabata. A boy will wake you and bring you tea in the morning.

KAWABATA: Uh—thank you.

[*She opens the door.*]

WOMAN: Listen.

KAWABATA: Listen?

WOMAN: To the waves. And the wind. [*Silence*] Good night, Mr. Kawabata.

[*He walks in. She closes the door. She moves to the table, begins cleaning up the tiles, as* LIGHTS FADE TO BLACK.]

Scene 2

Following evening. BEFORE THE LIGHTS COME UP, *we see a flame.* LIGHTS UP. *She sits at the desk. He is burning his record from yesterday, tosses it into the furnace.*

KAWABATA: I'm not a teacher, madame. I'm a writer.

WOMAN: Oh. A writer?

KAWABATA: Have you read my novels, short stories?

WOMAN: Have you ever been published in this?

KAWABATA: *Shifuno Tomo?* Trash.

WOMAN: Then I haven't read you.

KAWABATA: I don't write about beauty tips *or* American movie stars.

WOMAN: So you're going to write a report on us.

KAWABATA: I'm not a reporter. I write stories, novels. For some time now, I've been thinking about old men. How it must—

WOMAN: If you wish to write your report, Mr. Kawabata, you must realize the consequences of your actions. You understand, don't you, that we can't let the outside know we're here. That would mean the end of the house.

KAWABATA: And that should worry me?

WOMAN: Does it? Didn't you sleep well?

KAWABATA: Hardly. I was afraid to touch the covers and disturb her. I studied the walls until I fell asleep, watched the colors change in the dark.

WOMAN: I see.

KAWABATA: But what I've learned about the state to which men come—to think they return—night after night—for that.

WOMAN: Then why have *you* returned?

KAWABATA: Me?

WOMAN: Why didn't you just write your report and destroy the house?

KAWABATA: Story. I wanted...to burn that.

WOMAN: Is that all?

KAWABATA: Yes. That's all. [*He chuckles.*] I certainly have no desire to repeat last night's experience. It's been so many years since I've had to share a bed. No room to stretch.

WOMAN: Well, then, go.

KAWABATA: What?

WOMAN: If you've done what you've come for, then you must want to leave.

KAWABATA: Yes. I will. But first, I thought I might talk...to you.

WOMAN: What about? You've burned your record, you're no longer a guest, you plan to write your report without concern for the house, my girls, or myself.

KAWABATA: Yourself?

WOMAN: Our relationship is hardly suited to polite conversation.

KAWABATA: You will be all right.

WOMAN: "All right." How can you be so insensitive? You talk like a man who lives in other men's beds.

KAWABATA: You are very defiant, madame. Defiance is admirable in a woman. Defiance in a man is nothing more than a trained response, since we always expect to get our way. But a woman's defiance is her own.

WOMAN: Mr. Kawabata, you must not write this report.

KAWABATA: What if I do?

WOMAN: Then my life is over.

KAWABATA: Don't be melodramatic.

WOMAN: Please. Don't talk of things you know nothing about. I can tell you. Only one other time—twenty years ago—have I ever misjudged a guest. He came back the next evening, as you have tonight, and informed me he was...with the authorities. Then he left. I didn't know what to do. First, I tried to imagine all the awful things that could happen, hoping that by picturing them, I would prevent them from taking place, since real life never happens like we envision it will. Finally, after an hour of this, I decided to sleep. As I lay in bed, I began to wonder, what else could I do? where else could I go? I saw myself being carried up to Mount Obasute. My girls were carrying me up. "You're old now, Mama!" they cried. "We'll join your bones when we ourselves become old!" They left me in a cave and danced a *bon-odori* down the mountain, singing "Tokyo Ondo" as they went. [*She sings a little of it.*] I thought, "Look at them dancing. That's why I'm here and they're leaving me. Anyone who can dance down the mountain is free to go." And the next thing I knew, I was dancing a *bon-odori* right up there, on my bed—the springs making the sounds young people make in beds. And I danced down the hall to a telephone, and began looking for a new house for my girls. [*Pause*] That was twenty years ago. Look at me today. I can't even raise a foot for three seconds, let alone dance. I'm old, and I have no savings, no money, no skills. This time, Mr. Kawabata, I would have to stay on Mount Obasute.

KAWABATA: Look, madame, even if I wrote this story, it's possible that your house wouldn't be affected.

WOMAN: Why? Don't people read them?

KAWABATA: Of course. But people will likely think it's all from my head. You haven't read my stories. Like what you said to me—"Listen to the waves," you said.

WOMAN: They often help men sleep.

KAWABATA: In one of my novels, the boy always makes love to the woman while listening to the waves. The critics would probably laugh, "Old Kawabata and waves. Can't he think of anything new?"

WOMAN: And if the authorities—some of whom already suspect our existence—if they read your story, that won't make them certain? [*Pause*] What is that story to you?

KAWABATA: I want to write this story. I can do it, I know. I haven't written a story in...in...

WOMAN: That's just one story to you. This is my life.

KAWABATA: Better if you were rid of it.

WOMAN: Then you must change the facts—

KAWABATA: You made a mistake, madame.

WOMAN: —confuse the authorities.

KAWABATA: You chose not to cooperate with me yesterday.

WOMAN: But even that—

KAWABATA: You thought I was like the rest of them.

WOMAN: No, you mustn't write this report.

KAWABATA: You misjudged me. Now you see I'm different.

WOMAN: Yes, you are a reporter.

KAWABATA: You should have just told me about the house.

WOMAN: Mr. Kawabata—

KAWABATA: But you assumed—

WOMAN: —think of the girls.

KAWABATA: The girls?

WOMAN: The money they receive here.

KAWABATA: You shame them.

WOMAN: They are from poor families.

KAWABATA: They would be better off—

WOMAN: They come of their own will.

KAWABATA: —doing—working at . . . any other job.

WOMAN: And the old men.

KAWABATA: Don't tell me that.

WOMAN: We care about them. Look at this.

KAWABATA: At what?

WOMAN: At what you'll destroy.

KAWABATA: You humiliate them. Their despair—
it's so great.

WOMAN: What do you know?

KAWABATA: Your girls—are they all still virgins?

WOMAN: Was yours?

KAWABATA: Yes. Do you see the depth of the old
men's despair?

WOMAN: How do you know?

KAWABATA: That they can't even find the man-
hood to—

WOMAN: Mr. Kawabata, how do you know she was
still a virgin?

[*Pause.*]

KAWABATA: Don't worry. I didn't . . . molest her. I
walked into the room. I didn't believe she was
going to be naked. I knew you'd told me, but I
thought, no, you couldn't go that far, it would
be unfair to give men exactly what they want.
But she was lying on her back, the blanket
leaving bare two white shoulders and her neck.
I couldn't see clearly yet, so I ran my fingers
from one shoulder, across her neck, to the other
shoulder. Nothing blocked my finger's path—
nothing, no straps, only taut, smooth skin. I
still couldn't believe it, so I placed my index

finger at the base of her throat and moved down, under the blanket, further and further down— one unbroken line—all the way. When I knew, I pulled my hand away. She moaned and turned away from me. I looked at my finger, placed it at the top of her spine and followed the hard bumps all the way down. I looked at my finger again, tasted it. Then I placed it against the back of her knee, under her nostrils, behind her ear, in the hair under her arm. And every place my finger touched, it pressed. And everywhere it pressed, her skin resisted with the same soft strength and I thought, "This...is youth."...I lay down and buried my nose against her scalp, my nose rubbing up and down as her foot rubbed against the sheets. When I woke up, it was just past dawn. The room was bright. That's when I tried to assault her—yes, it's true, I *tried*. But I'm an honorable man, so don't worry for her. If I had known she was a virgin, I would never have even thought of it to begin with.

[*Pause.*]

WOMAN: Well, this is too bad. You know the rules of the house, don't you?

KAWABATA: Yes.

WOMAN: But still...

KAWABATA: But I didn't.

WOMAN: Very technical.

KAWABATA: I don't know why. It was too bright in the room. I became sad, then angry. I wanted to hit her or something. But instead, I tried that instead.

WOMAN: Can I get you some tea?

KAWABATA: Huh? Yes, please. Thank you.

WOMAN: Why do you do that kind of thing anyway?

KAWABATA: I told you, I don't know. And don't
make it sound like I do it often.

WOMAN: No, I mean about sleeping with your head
in her hair.

KAWABATA: Oh, that.

WOMAN: Don't you worry about suffocating?

KAWABATA: I have my reasons.

WOMAN: Well, go on. There's very little you can't
tell me now.

[*Pause.*]

KAWABATA: Her hair—the girl last night. It had
a special smell. Like an old lady friend of mine.

WOMAN: Your wife?

KAWABATA: No, I'm afraid not. Maybe thirty years
ago. She was married to—oh, some kind of
Hong Kong businessman, maybe even a movie
producer—I can't remember. I do remember
she lived alone with her servants—he was
always away—in a huge castle in Kowloon.
It really was—a castle in Kowloon. I didn't
know they had castles either. Where did we
meet? Kyoto? I can't—you see, I'd even forgotten her until I smelled that girl's hair. My
lady friend, I'd smell her hair and she'd cry,
"Don't do that. It's filthy!" But I'd smell her
hair for hours. I wonder what she's doing now,
She was the only woman who ever winked at
me.

WOMAN: Mr. Kawabata...

KAWABATA: I was shocked. This was many years
ago, you know—huh?

WOMAN: I apologize. For my hysteria.

KAWABATA: Have you...seen my point?

WOMAN: Yes.

KAWABATA: About the story? My writing?

WOMAN: Yes. Would you like to be our guest again tonight?

KAWABATA: What? Even after—?

WOMAN: I misjudged you. You are honest. That's a rare quality. I was irrational. This time, no charge. Only please stay.

KAWABATA: I came here to burn my record.

WOMAN: We can make you a new one. The girl I've picked out for you tonight is more experienced than the one before.

KAWABATA: It's not the same one?

WOMAN: No. Isn't it better to have a different one?

KAWABATA: You understand that I won't...do anything like...last night.

WOMAN: Of course, Mr. Kawabata. I see you're a gentleman after all. Your sleeping medicine?

KAWABATA: My— Oh, thank you. I don't quite understand.

WOMAN: Don't understand. Just enjoy tonight's sleep. May I help you undress?

KAWABATA: Thank you. I suppose...I can't refuse your generosity.

WOMAN: Thank you.

[*They are behind the screen.*]

KAWABATA: Uh—where was your house located before?

WOMAN: Before? We've always been here.

KAWABATA: No, but that story you told. The one about your guest the policeman.

WOMAN: Oh, that.

KAWABATA: Where did you move from?

WOMAN: We didn't. [*Pause*] Things just worked out.
   [*They come out. She opens the door, gives him
   a key.*] Third door on your left. This one's even
   prettier—and more experienced.
KAWABATA: What do you mean, more experienced? After all, she's sound asleep.
WOMAN: Good night, Mr. Kawabata.
   [*He goes in. She closes the door. She returns to
   the desk, pulls out her record book, and begins
   to write.* LIGHTS TO BLACK.]

Scene 3

Several months later. KAWABATA, *sitting alone. Silence.* WOMAN *enters from door to rooms.*

WOMAN: Yes, I can arrange something tonight.
   [*Pause*] But you should know better. You've been
   a guest for five months now. Why didn't you
   call first, instead of just bursting in?
KAWABATA: [*Sharply*] I'm sorry!
WOMAN: It will be a few minutes before things are
   ready.
   [*Pause.*]
KAWABATA: Can you give me some of that sleeping
   medicine?
WOMAN: Now? Well, if you like.
KAWABATA: No, not that. The kind you give the
   girls.

WOMAN: The girls?

KAWABATA: Yes. I want to sleep as deeply as they do.

WOMAN: Sir, that kind of medicine isn't healthy for old men.

KAWABATA: I can take it. I'm your guest, aren't I? You always say so. You always say you want to serve your guests, don't you?

WOMAN: What's wrong with this?

KAWABATA: I wake up. I wake up at two, three in the morning. Sometimes, it takes me an hour to fall back to sleep. I just lie there.

WOMAN: Your body shouldn't be building up resistance.

KAWABATA: That's not it.

WOMAN: If you're tired of my girls, I can arrange something special.

KAWABATA: Will it help me sleep? [*Pause*] See? Whatever you do with the girls—it doesn't matter if I have to lie there like a stone.

WOMAN: Is there a girl here you'd like to see again?

KAWABATA: No. It's not the girls, it's me. When I began coming here, I'd lie awake at nights, too, but I'd love it, because I'd remember...things I'd forgotten for years—women, romances. I stopped writing—even exercises—it all seemed so pointless. But these last few weeks, I smell their skin, run my fingers between their toes—there's nothing there but skin and toes. I wake up in the middle of the night, and all I can remember was what it was like to remember, and I'm a prisoner in that bed.

WOMAN: I'm sorry. I can't—

KAWABATA: No. Listen. It's getting worse. Last

night, when I woke up, all I could think of was the death of my friend.

WOMAN: I'm sorry.

KAWABATA: I hadn't thought of Mishima's suicide in a year. But last night—it began again—what must it have been like? [*Pause*] *Hara-kiri*. How does a man you know commit *hara-kiri*? A loved one, a friend. Strangers, of course. They kill themselves daily. But someone you know—how do they find that will? [*Pause*] The will. To feel your hands forcing steel through your stomach and if the hands stopped the pain would stop, but the hands keep going. They must become another being, your hands. Yes. Your hands become another being and the steel becomes you.

WOMAN: You shouldn't give your friend more respect than he deserves.

KAWABATA: He was a man, though. He had his lover stand behind him and chop off his head when the cutting was done.

WOMAN: I'm not going to give you dangerous drugs. I'm sorry. [*Pause*] Don't worry so much about your friend, Mr. Kawabata. People commit suicide for themselves. That's one thing I know. I had a sister, Mr. Kawabata. My parents sent her away to Tokyo, hoping that she would be trained in the tea, the dance, the *koto,* to attract a man of wealth. I wept with envy at the fine material Mother bought for her kimonos—gold thread, brocade. The day she left, I was angry—she was crying at her good fortune. Years went by; we were both engaged. She came back from Tokyo for her wedding and we could barely rec-

ognize her—she had neither the hands nor the
speech of anyone we knew. I got very angry at
her haughtiness—my chore was to pick the
maggots from the rice, and I purposely left a
few in, hoping she would get them... Their
wedding was the most beautiful I'd ever seen.
Just before she was to leave, my sister cornered
me outside, tears streaming down her face, and
begged my forgiveness... They tried to keep the
story a secret from us, but, well... such a ro-
mantic story; the stuff legends are made of. It
seems my sister had a lover in the village, that
they had pledged fidelity long before she left
for Tokyo. The next morning, my father went
to draw water from the well. In the dim light
before dawn, two faces came rushing up to the
water's surface. Two faces—my sister and my
fiancé... So don't worry about your friend, Mr.
Kawabata. People kill themselves to save
themselves, not others. [*Pause*] Now, I'm going
to prepare something special. There will be two
girls. There will be twice the warmth.

[*She exits. He goes to the cabinet, takes out the
vials and a cup. He pours and drinks three
glasses of the sleeping potion. He returns the
items. She reenters.*]

KAWABATA: Madame?

WOMAN: Yes.

KAWABATA: If I were to commit *hara-kiri,* would
you chop off my head?

WOMAN: Mr. Kawabata—

KAWABATA: No. Answer me. If I gave you a sword—
I'd pay you, you know—I wouldn't expect you
to do it for nothing.

WOMAN: This type of question doesn't help either of us.

KAWABATA: Listen—would you chop off my head when I whispered, "Now. Please. Now." Or would you walk away laughing, counting your change?

WOMAN: Will you stop that? Will you stop that selfishness?

KAWABATA: No, the question is—answer it!—would you chop—

WOMAN: No! No! That's *your* question, yours only. You never think of anyone else's suffering— you're so self-centered, all you men, every last one of you. Have some woman chop off your head, leave her alone, do you think of her? She takes her few dollars, she buys some vegetables, she eats them and slowly withers away— no glory, no honor, just a slow fading into the background—that's all you expect. No. Mr. Kawabata, if *I* wanted to commit *hara-kiri,* would you chop off *my* head?

KAWABATA: Women don't commit *hara-kiri.*

WOMAN: What if I did? What if I were the first?

KAWABATA: This is pointless.

WOMAN: I know—you think I would do it the woman's way, just slipping the tiny knife in here. But what if I wanted to do it like a man? Completely. Powerfully.

KAWABATA: That's a foolish question.

WOMAN: I would do it better than you.

KAWABATA: Don't be absurd.

WOMAN: I would be braver.

KAWABATA: What a ridiculous notion!

WOMAN: If you didn't chop off my head, I'd be glad

KAWABATA: This is a waste of time.

WOMAN: Because then, I'd be braver than you or your friend.

KAWABATA: Don't blaspheme Mishima.

WOMAN: I'd die like the generals.

KAWABATA: You're just an old woman.

WOMAN: I'd be the old woman who died like the generals.

KAWABATA: Show some respect.

[*Pause.*]

WOMAN: So quiet now, aren't you, Mr. Kawabata. Why don't you spout glorious phrases about chopping off my head? [*Pause*] Or why don't you write your report and destroy us all? [*Pause*] Your room is ready. Should I help you undress?

KAWABATA: No.

[*He starts to leave, still dressed.*]

WOMAN: Don't forget your key.

[*He returns, takes the key.*]

WOMAN: Fourth door on your right.

[*He exits. She closes the door. Pause. She goes to her desk, takes out a make-up kit. She stands next to the mirror, powders her face completely white, does her eyes, her mouth. She then goes to the door to the rooms, pulls up a chair, and sits facing it.*]

KAWABATA: [*Offstage*] Madame! Madame!

[*He enters, wearing only his pants. He is in a panic, but the large amount of sleeping potion he's taken has started to take effect. He stares at her. She says nothing. He is speechless. Long pause.*]

WOMAN: Go back to bed. There is still the other girl.

KAWABATA: Your...one of your girls. She's...not
breathing. No pulse.

WOMAN: Her body is being removed even as you
speak. Now go back to bed. There is still the
other girl.

KAWABATA: Other girl?

WOMAN: Yes, there were two, remember?

KAWABATA: I can't...your face. Why is it that way?
I can't go back in there. She's dead. Do something. Go in.

WOMAN: Very little I can do. She took too much of
her sleeping medicine, I think.

KAWABATA: This is inhuman.

WOMAN: It's difficult, but these things happen.

KAWABATA: This is...not human.

WOMAN: Now, go back. It won't do to be walking
the streets at this hour.

KAWABATA: Why do people come here? Why don't
they leave? I won't...I'm leaving.

WOMAN: You can't leave.

KAWABATA: I'm leaving. Where's my shirt, my
coat?

WOMAN: Where will you go?

KAWABATA: Out. Home.

WOMAN: In your condition? Look at you—what
happened, anyway?

KAWABATA: No, I don't care. I'll sleep in the streets.

WOMAN: You'll die in the cold, that's what you'll
do.

KAWABATA: Yes. I'll die in the cold. I'll die in the
cold before I become like Old Eguchi. Look at
him—pathetic—here every damn night.

WOMAN: Like Old Eguchi? How are you *not* like
Old Eguchi?

KAWABATA: I can still sleep somewhere else.

WOMAN: Today, perhaps. Tomorrow, no.

KAWABATA: Where's my shirt?

WOMAN: Here. [*She leads him to the mirror.*] Look at yourself. Even as we speak, the lines are getting deeper, the hair is getting thinner, your lips are getting drier. Even as we speak, the shape of your face is changing, and with it, a mind, a will, as different as the face. You can leave now, Mr. Kawabata, but as much as you deny it, your face will continue to change, as if your will didn't even exist. See my face? Look at it. Close. I try and powder it like a young girl. But look—all that's here is an obscene mockery of youth. Don't be like this, Mr. Kawabata. Go back to sleep and let's not hear any more of your grandstanding.

[KAWABATA *is firmly in the grip of the drug now.*]

KAWABATA: I'm . . . so tired. I drank too much of the potion.

WOMAN: That? I'm sorry. My fault. I shouldn't have left it there. Well, you should be all right. That's not as strong as the stuff you wanted.

KAWABATA: I would leave, I would, you know.

WOMAN: But you're too tired?

KAWABATA: I'm not coming back.

WOMAN: Of course not. Here. I'll help you to your room.

[*She starts to sing the "Tokyo Ondo" softly as they exit together.* LIGHTS FADE SLOWLY, *and we can still hear the song.*]

Scene 4

A week later. Evening. He is alone in the room. He is wrapping something in a small box. He completes the wrapping, puts the box into the breast pocket of the suit he is wearing. She enters from the door to the rooms. She carries a manuscript.

WOMAN: You've sent this to your publisher?

KAWABATA: Yes. It will be in print in time.
[*Pause.*]

WOMAN: You go very easy on yourself.

KAWABATA: In what sense?

WOMAN: You don't even name the main character after yourself. You call him old Eguchi.

KAWABATA: Maybe I'm writing about him, not me.

WOMAN: And here...this story. That never happened. No man ever died here.

KAWABATA: Are you sure?

WOMAN: Who told you that?

KAWABATA: No one. I just thought...maybe.

WOMAN: And look at this. All this talk about the girls with their electric blankets. We don't even have electric blankets.

KAWABATA: Madame, I write stories, not newspaper copy. I don't—

WOMAN: This woman—she's very...uh...she seems so hard.

KAWABATA: The story's not about her.

WOMAN: She has no feelings, no heart. She's

198

so...above it all, like she never cries, like her heart has gone through life without stumbling. She's like a ghost that walks through men's houses without creaking the floorboards.

KAWABATA: It's rather depersonalized, objective...

WOMAN: "Objective"? How can you say that? Look at the end—here—when the girl dies—like last week—and she says, "There's still the other girl." Doesn't that make her just one kind of woman?

KAWABATA: What I mean is that—

WOMAN: Doesn't it? Yes, I said that. But I shared things with you, stories. I let you see me ridiculous, hideous, a fool in my powder. Where is that? Is this all you remember? Just an old, cruel woman who serves you tea and takes your money?

KAWABATA: You have to understand...the joy was that I could finally write again at all.

WOMAN: Yes. That is surprising.

KAWABATA: I wasn't going to stop it.

WOMAN: I was surprised we hadn't seen you all week.

KAWABATA: Do you understand?

WOMAN: Do you still think that the house will survive this story? Even after revealing the girl's death?

KAWABATA: I don't know. Who can say?

WOMAN: You didn't change anything, make it harder for them to find us.

KAWABATA: I'm sorry. I wanted to, but I couldn't. I'm sorry.

WOMAN: No. Sorry has nothing to do with it. We each do our work.

KAWABATA: When I told you last week—drugged—that I wasn't coming back again, did you believe me?

WOMAN: Of course not. But there was a part of me...Up to a point, you'd acted like all my guests. The game with the tiles, being unable to assault my girl when you found her a virgin, you fit right into the gentleman's pattern. But your memories—leaving you so soon. There was a part of me that wondered. I wanted to call you. Once I even finished dialing your number. But I hung up before it rang. I sat here and thought up tortures for you. I thought you'd gone away...committed *hara-kiri,* and that you were waiting for me to come and chop off your head. I decided to stay right here.

KAWABATA: Did you think I wasn't coming back?

WOMAN: After a time, I began to wonder. [*Pause. She goes to the mirror, looks at it.*] Well, there're many things I could do now. I could move to another city. Try to start again, from the ground. Or I could sit here, the same as always. Who knows? Perhaps no one will believe your story.

KAWABATA: That's quite possible. I've told you that.

WOMAN: Which would you recommend?

KAWABATA: Me? I don't know what kind of risks you take, or what's involved in starting over.

WOMAN: No. You don't.

KAWABATA: I think, though, that at our age, starting again is only worthwhile if one enjoys the process.

WOMAN: "At our age"?

KAWABATA: It's—uh—difficult to make long-range plans, you know.

WOMAN: Since when are we the same age?

KAWABATA: We are, aren't we?

WOMAN: Yes, we are.

KAWABATA: Give or take five years—

WOMAN: And you, then—

KAWABATA: —which hardly matters at this point.

WOMAN: —what will you do? Will you come back here?

KAWABATA: No.

WOMAN: Oh.

KAWABATA: No. My life becomes very simple now. [*He takes out a packet of bills, offers them to her.*] Here. Here. Take it. Enough for you to...I don't know, buy a new house, anywhere you want. Or retire. Yes, retire and never worry about a thing again.

WOMAN: This is...so much...amazing. I can't take this. Why?

KAWABATA: I want you to serve me.

WOMAN: This is...an outrageous amount, Mr. Kawabata. I cannot accept it.

KAWABATA: Please. You'll need the money. An even trade.

WOMAN: Do you want a girl? A room?

KAWABATA: No.

WOMAN: I can fix you something special.

KAWABATA: Fix me some tea.

WOMAN: Oh, I forgot. I'm sorry.

KAWABATA: No. Don't apologize.

WOMAN: I'm sorry. So rude of me. It's such a cold night.

KAWABATA: You make very wonderful tea.

WOMAN: No, it's not.

KAWABATA: Yes.

WOMAN: It's nothing.

[*Pause.*]

KAWABATA: I've grown in this house.

WOMAN: You feel young here?

KAWABATA: I did. As I've slept here, I've grown older. I've seen my sweethearts, my wife, my mistresses, my daughters, until there's only one thing left. [*She comes with the tea.*] Will you powder your face again?

WOMAN: Mr. Kawabata, don't—

KAWABATA: Please.

WOMAN: You're mocking me—an old woman.

KAWABATA: No, I've brought you something. [*He reaches into a bag he is carrying, pulls out a kimono.*]

WOMAN: Oh!

KAWABATA: Yes. Take it.

WOMAN: It's...No, this isn't for me.

KAWABATA: Yes. See? Gold thread. Brocade.

WOMAN: I can't accept this. Please. Give it to someone who deserves it.

KAWABATA: It's for you.

WOMAN: One of your young admirers. You are a famous writer. You must have many.

KAWABATA: Please. Put it on. It's just like the one you told me about.

WOMAN: It's gorgeous, too beautiful—

KAWABATA: Put it on and powder your face.

WOMAN: You're so foolish, Mr. Kawabata. I'll disgrace these clothes. Once they drape down my old bones, especially with my face in that powder, they'll change into something else completely, believe me.

KAWABATA: Don't be shy. You'll do me a great honor to wear my gift.
[*Pause.*]

WOMAN: If you insist.

KAWABATA: Yes. Please. [*She starts to leave.*] No. Please. Do it in here. I want to watch.

WOMAN: Women don't like men to watch them making up.

[*Pause. She sits, begins making up.*]

KAWABATA: I finished that story several days ago, you know. It came out of me like a wild animal, my hands were cramping at the pen. I wanted to show it to you while it was still warm, but I kept turning back. It's the same way I've felt before when I've written the end of a story, yet known that the story had more to do before I could rest. So I trusted my instincts—I watched television for two full days, since usually, what hasn't yet been revealed will rise to the surface in its own time. Yesterday, I woke up and knew what had to be added, and words weren't the question at all, so I sent the manuscript as it was to my publisher and went out shopping.

WOMAN: For the kimono? It's so beautiful.

KAWABATA: I tried to imagine the one you described.

WOMAN: This is every bit as beautiful.

KAWABATA: It's not the same?

WOMAN: It's difficult for me to remember. I was so young. But my sister's couldn't have been any finer.

[*She takes the kimono, goes behind the screen, begins changing into it. He takes the small box out of his breast pocket, removes his jacket, takes off his tie, unbuttons his collar, takes off his shoes. Finally, she speaks.*]

WOMAN: After the war, when we realized Father

wasn't coming back, and the family was dispersed, I moved here to Tokyo. And I thought, "Now I'll dress in brocade also. I'll wear gold threads, too." But when I remembered my sister, I lost any desire to have anything like that. It's just as well, that being after the war and all. And I've never had the money, even to this day—ai! You'd think at my age, I'd have earned the right to stop worrying about money.

KAWABATA: But I've given you your security.

WOMAN: Yes, yes. I still can't— But why? [*She steps out from behind the screen.*] See? Don't I look hideous?

KAWABATA: You're exactly what I want.

WOMAN: Is this what you want? An old hag pretending to be young again?

KAWABATA: Please. Sit down.

WOMAN: The tea—it's probably cold.

KAWABATA: No, it's fine. Open that box.

WOMAN: This one?

KAWABATA: Yes.

WOMAN: It's beautifully wrapped.

[*She starts to open it.*]

KAWABATA: It took me several hours to buy the kimono, and the rest of the day to buy that.

[*She removes a vial of clear liquid.*]

KAWABATA: Please. Add it to the tea. [*Pause*] Go on. You said it was all right for us to bring our own medicine, didn't you? [*Pause*] The top lifts off. [*Pause*] Don't worry. I'm not going to ask you to drink it or anything. It's for me. Now, go on.

WOMAN: Respect me, Mr. Kawabata.

KAWABATA: I do.

WOMAN: Tell me—this isn't a sleeping potion.

KAWABATA: No.

WOMAN: Do you want a room?

KAWABATA: No.

WOMAN: I want to give you one. Free.

KAWABATA: I've already paid.

WOMAN: For what?

KAWABATA: Paid not to have a room.

WOMAN: For me?

KAWABATA: Please, empty the vial.

WOMAN: No.

[*Pause.*]

KAWABATA: Isn't this your job? Isn't this what you get paid to do? For your life's security, madame, you should be willing to endure a little more than usual. [*Pause*] What's the matter? I thought of all people in the world, you would understand this. [*Silence. She empties the vial into the pot.*] Good. I'm sorry. I didn't mean to do that, say those things. But I assume... we have an understanding. Do we?

WOMAN: Look at me. See this? [*Her face*] This? [*Her dress*] That should answer your question. What should I do now?

KAWABATA: Tell me again, why I should come to your house.

WOMAN: [*As before*] Our guests sleep very well here. It's the warmth, they say.

KAWABATA: Warmth?

WOMAN: Our guests are not afraid to sleep at night. The darkness does not threaten them.

KAWABATA: Oh, it's so cold tonight. Look at my hand. Could you pour me some tea, please? [*Pause.*]

WOMAN: Yes. Certainly. [*She does; her eyes are fixed on him. She watches him drink as she*

speaks.] The girl I've picked out for you
is...she's...half Japanese, half Caucasian, very
beautiful, like a child, like a pearly-white snow-
flake child, whose foot never—always—moves,
traces circles around the snow—uh—sheet,
fleeing—uh—feeling the warmth, the heart—
uh—the heat, finding it, the warmth, the
heart—uh—the heat, taking it, the warmth, the
heat, always...

[*He puts down the cup. It is empty. Pause. She
refills his cup. It sits on the table, untouched.
Silence.*]

KAWABATA: Now, we are as we should be.

WOMAN: Yes, I suppose so.

KAWABATA: And you look so beautiful.

WOMAN: Don't be cruel.

KAWABATA: But you do.

WOMAN: I won't listen.

KAWABATA: If we were thirty, maybe even twenty
years younger, who knows?

WOMAN: Mr. Kawabata, for so long now, you've
been trying to show me that you're different
from my other guests.

KAWABATA: I'm sorry.

WOMAN: No, no, you've done it. You've gotten your
wish. How does it make you feel?

KAWABATA: I wasted so much time.

WOMAN: You've proven to me that you're a thousand times more terrible and wonderful than
any of my other guests.

KAWABATA: How sad. I don't even care about that
anymore. If I'm different, it's only because I
believed you when you showed me that I was
the same as the rest of them. [*Pause*] It's funny.

I've known you all this time, and I don't even know your name.

WOMAN: Michiko.

KAWABATA: Michiko. Wonderful. You have the hands of a young woman, did you know that, Michiko?

WOMAN: No. My hands are ugly.

KAWABATA: Let me see them, Michiko.

WOMAN: They are the hands of a crow.

KAWABATA: Please. Let me see them. [*She does.*] Amazing. And you—from the country. [*He touches them.*] They are long. And firm. And warm with blood. [*He kisses them.*] I'm starting to become tired. May I rest in your lap? [*She nods.*] Thank you, Michiko. [*Silently, she begins to stroke his hair.*] You've been very kind for allowing me to...take these liberties with you. I'm sorry I said those things about you. But I was afraid that you weren't as strong as I expected, that you couldn't give me what I needed. I shouldn't have doubted. [*Pause*] Please. Take the money. Be happy. Enjoy these last years. Buy what you've always wanted. [*Pause*] I do want you to take care of yourself. [*Silence*] You can't believe what a comfort it is for me to be falling asleep, yet able to open my eyes, look up, and see you.

[*His eyes are closed. She looks around the house, continues to stroke his hair. She begins to sing the "Tokyo Ondo" as a lullaby.*]

[*She picks up the remaining cup of tea, drinks it.*]

[*She resumes singing, strokes his hair, as lights* FADE TO BLACK.]

CURTAIN

BARD BOOKS
DISTINGUISHED DRAMA